Her Fragra

It was the one he remembered from that night in his car—the night that had changed everything.

He'd wanted Angie Montoya from the first time he'd seen her with his brother. He'd wanted her that night, and, damn his soul, he wanted her now.

"Jordan…" Her lush lips shaped his name. "I need…"

He silenced her with a gentle kiss. As her mouth opened in invitation, the kiss deepened. She moaned and stretched on tiptoe to lift her hips closer to his erection. Jordan hauled her upward, grinding her against him. She was gasping by the time he found the zipper at the back of her dress.

That night in the car, they'd managed to stop before things got out of control.

But there would be no stopping now.

Dear Reader,

Welcome to my very first Harlequin Desire novel. After a long line of historicals, I'm thrilled to be lending a new voice to these powerful, passionate stories.

While writing this book, I fell in love with my characters. Fiercely independent, Angie carried on when the death of her fiancé left her alone and pregnant. Now, as she struggles to raise her son, can she find happiness with a former enemy—the twin brother of the man she loved?

Jordan had long believed Angie was after his brother's money. Now her young son, Lucas, is the only surviving link to his twin—and the heir to Justin's fortune. Jordan is determined to raise the boy as his own. But proud, stubborn Angie is part of the package—and he can't stop thinking about her.

One of my favorite characters has no lines to speak. He's a rescue dog, saved from death row by the love of a little boy. I'm hoping Rudy's story will inspire someone out there to adopt a homeless pet or support a group that works to help these innocent animals.

Before closing, I'd like to thank two of the people who made this book possible—Desire senior editor Stacy Boyd for taking a chance on "something different," and my wonderful editor Elizabeth Mazer, whose patience and encouragement got me this far and whose gifted touch added the polish to make my story shine.

Love to you all. Enjoy.

Elizabeth

ELIZABETH LANE

IN HIS BROTHER'S PLACE

HARLEQUIN®

entertain, enrich, inspire™

Recycling programs
for this product may
not exist in your area.

ISBN-13: 978-0-373-73221-0

IN HIS BROTHER'S PLACE

www.Harlequin.com

Printed in U.S.A.

Books by Elizabeth Lane

Other titles by this author
available in ebook format.

ELIZABETH LANE

has lived and traveled in many parts of the world, including Europe, Latin America and the Far East, but her heart remains in the American West, where she was born and raised. Her idea of heaven is hiking a mountain trail on a clear autumn day. She also enjoys music, animals and dancing. You can learn more about Elizabeth by visiting her website at www.elizabethlaneauthor.com.

One

Santa Fe, New Mexico

"You're sure about the boy—and his mother?" Jordan's grip tightened on the phone.

"You're the one who has to be sure, Mr. Cooper." The private investigator's voice was as flat as a digitized recording. "The packet's on its way to your ranch by courier—birth certificate, hospital records, the mother's address and several discreet photos. Once you've seen everything, you can draw your own conclusion. If you need follow-up—"

"No, there'll be nothing else. I'll transfer your fee as soon as I've seen the documents."

Jordan ended the call with a click. The packet would be arriving from Albuquerque within the hour. If his hunch was right, it would hold enough legal and emotional dynamite to blast his well-ordered world into chaos.

Stepping away from the desk, he stared out the window of his study, which commanded a vista of open ranchland stretching toward the horizon. In the distance, the Sangre de Cristo Mountains, rich with autumn color, glimmered in the November sunlight. This was Cooper land, as it had been for more than a hundred years. When his mother died it would pass to him as the sole surviving heir of the family trust. He was the last Cooper heir— or so he'd thought. But if the report confirmed what he suspected…

Jordan turned away from the window, leaving the thought unfinished. It wasn't too late to back off, he reminded himself. When the packet arrived, he could burn the damned thing unopened or shove it through the shredder. But he'd only be destroying paper. Nothing could erase the memory of Angelina Montoya or change the reality of what she'd done to his family.

Especially now.

Jordan's eyes shifted toward the far wall, bare except for a group of framed family photos. The largest showed two young men grinning over a stringer of freshly caught rainbow trout. Their features were so nearly identical that a visitor would've been hard pressed to tell which was Jordan and which was his twin brother, Justin.

When the picture was taken the two had still been close. Three years later, Justin had fallen for dark-eyed Angie Montoya, hostess in an upscale Mexican restaurant off the Plaza. His determination to marry her had torn the family apart.

Convinced the woman was a gold digger, Jordan and his parents had taken every action they could think of to separate the couple. The resulting schism between the brothers had never had a chance to heal. Rushing home from a ski trip on the eve of Angie's birthday, Justin had flown his Cirrus SR22 plane into a storm and crashed into a Utah mountain.

Grief had dragged Jordan's father into an early grave and made a bitter old woman of his mother. As for Angie Montoya, she had simply vanished—until last week when, after nearly four years, Jordan had come across her name. Searching further, he'd found a picture that had him on the phone within the hour with the best private investigator in the state. He'd wanted answers, and now he was about to get them. The report would almost surely confirm what Jordan had suspected.

Angelina Montoya had not only stolen Justin from his family—she had stolen Justin's son.

Albuquerque

"You've been working hard on that picture, Lucas." Angie swiveled her chair away from the bedroom computer hutch to give her son her full attention. "Why don't you tell me about it?"

Lucas held out the drawing—three lopsided stick figures sketched in crayon on a sheet of copy paper. "It's our family. This short one is me. This one with long black hair is you."

"And who's this, up here at the top?" Anticipating the answer, Angie felt her throat tighten.

"That's Daddy, up in heaven. He's looking out for us, just like you said."

"That's right. Do you want to put this picture on the fridge to remind us?"

"Okay." Clutching his masterpiece, the boy scampered down the hall toward the tiny kitchen. Angie gulped back a surge of emotion. It wasn't easy, living with daily reminders of Justin. But she'd wanted to make sure Lucas didn't feel fatherless. She kept Justin's framed portrait at the boy's bedside and an album of snapshots on the bookshelf, within his reach. His small fingers had worn the pages thin at the corners.

Most of the photos showed Justin and Angie together or Justin alone. There were no pictures of Justin's family. After the way they'd treated her, she wanted nothing to do with any of them—especially Jordan.

It was Jordan who'd come on her birthday to bring the news of Justin's death. He hadn't said much, but Jordan's manner had made his feelings clear. Weeks earlier, the family had offered her fifty thousand dollars to walk away from Justin. If she'd taken it, Justin would still be alive.

Angie would never forget the bitterness in those contemptuous gray eyes. How could two brothers who looked so much alike be so different? Justin had been warm and loving, quick to laugh and quick to forgive. The thought of Jordan conjured up words like *cold, judgmental, mercenary...*

And *manipulative.* She'd had firsthand experience with that particular trait of his.

The sound of the door buzzer broke into her thoughts. "I'll get it!" Lucas called.

"Stop right there, mister. You know better." Striding into the living room, she scooped him up in her arms. Their cramped two-bedroom apartment was affordable, but the neighborhood wasn't the best. When someone came to the door, Angie made it a rule to send Lucas to his room until she knew the situation was safe. Maybe by next year, if her web design business continued to grow, she'd have the money to rent a small house with a fenced yard. Until then...

The doorbell buzzed again, twice. Setting Lucas on

his play rug, Angie closed the bedroom door and hurried back down the hall. She didn't get many visitors here, and she certainly wasn't expecting company. Any unexpected knock tended to raise her suspicions.

Jordan tensed as the light, rapid footsteps approached. Seeing Angie again was bound to be awkward as hell. Maybe he should have sent somebody else first—someone who could assess the situation without putting the woman on her guard. But no, whatever waited on the other side of that door, he was duty-bound to face up to it. He needed to do the right thing—for his family legacy, for his brother's memory…even for Angie, if time had mellowed out her stubborn streak enough to let her see reason.

The dead bolt slid back. The latch clicked. Jordan held his breath as the door opened to the width allowed by the security chain.

Eyes the hue of rich black coffee stared up at him— eyes framed by lush, feathery lashes. Jordan had almost forgotten how stunning those eyes could be. He watched them widen, then narrow suspiciously.

"What do you want, Jordan?" Her husky little voice, taut with strain, pricked his memory.

"For starters, I'd like to come in."

"Why?" She made no move to unfasten the chain.

It seemed her stubborn streak hadn't mellowed in the slightest. "So I won't have to stand out here and talk to you through this blasted door."

"I can't imagine we'd have anything worth saying to each other."

Jordan's thin-drawn patience snapped. "You have a choice, Angie," he growled. "Let me in so we can talk like civilized people, or I'll shout loud enough to be heard all over the building. Either way, I'm not leaving until you hear what I came to say." He paused, reminding himself that it wouldn't do any good to threaten her. "Who knows," he added, "this might be something you'll want to hear."

He braced himself for a stinging retort. Instead, she simply closed the door. Jordan waited in the silence. Seconds crawled past before he heard the rattle of the chain. Slowly the door swung open.

He willed himself to look at the apartment first. The living room was bright and clean, the walls freshly painted, the slipcovered sofa decorated with red, blue and yellow cushions. But the place didn't look much bigger than one of Jordan's horse stalls. The building itself was run down with no security system at all—anyone could walk in off the street, as he had done. And he had seen what was outside—the loitering teens, the gang graffiti on the walls. If this was the best Angie could afford, she had to be struggling financially.

There was no sign of her son. Only a battered copy of *Goodnight Moon* on the coffee table betrayed the presence of a child in the apartment. She would've put the boy out of sight, of course. Maybe that was the reason she'd taken so long to undo the chain latch.

As he stepped inside, closing the door behind him, Angie moved into Jordan's line of vision. She was dressed in a simple black tee and faded jeans that fit her shapely body without being provocatively tight. Her dark hair fell past her shoulders in silky waves. Her feet were bare, the toenails painted a soft baby pink.

She was still seductively beautiful. But Jordan had been aware of that even before his brother fell in love with her—and afterward, too.

He braced himself against the replay of that unguarded moment in his car, the taste of her tears, the willing heat of her ripe mouth, the sinuous fit of her curves in his arms. It had been a mistake—one that hadn't been repeated. He'd done his best to block the memory. But forgetting a woman like Angie was easier said than done.

He cleared his throat. "Aren't you going to ask me to sit down?"

"There's room on the sofa." She was clearly ill at ease. He imagined she would have liked to settle herself in a chair on the other side of the room, but aside from the couch, there was nowhere else to sit other than the floor. After Jordan had taken his seat, she perched on the padded arm at the far end, her toes working their way beneath the seat cushion.

Jordan shifted his position to face her. She didn't trust him, and he couldn't blame her. But somehow he had to make her listen. He had to make this right—for Justin's sake.

If he could help his brother's son and the woman Justin had wanted for his wife, then maybe his brother's soul would forgive him…and perhaps someday, Jordan could forgive himself.

Jordan hadn't changed. Angie studied the frigid gray eyes, the pit bull set of his jaw, the unruly brown hair with the boyish cowlick at the crown. If he smiled he'd look a lot like Justin. But she'd hardly ever seen Jordan smile, at least not at her.

The sight of him had sent her pulse careening like a cornered animal's. Jordan had the face of the man she'd loved. But his heart was solid granite. If he'd taken the trouble to track her down, she could be sure it wasn't out of kindness.

"How did you find me?" she asked.

"Internet. Your name was on a web site you'd designed

for a printing business. Pure chance that it caught my eye, but after I saw it I was curious. I clicked through to your page and saw the photo of you working at your computer. I couldn't help noticing you weren't alone."

Angie's heart dropped as his words sank home. A neighbor had taken the picture. At the last second, Lucas had moved in so close that the lower edge of the frame showed the top of his head from the back.

A sick fear crept over her. She could have cropped the photo. Such a simple precaution. Why hadn't she done it? What had she been thinking?

But the picture couldn't have told Jordan enough to bring him here. Angie's temper flashed as the truth dawned. "You had me investigated, didn't you?"

His jaw tightened. "Where's the boy, Angie? Where's Lucas?"

"You have no right to ask!" She was on guard now, a tigress ready to strike in defense of her cub. "Lucas is my son. *My* son!"

"And my brother's son. I have a copy of the birth certificate. You listed Justin as the father. I'm assuming that's the truth."

Something crumbled inside her. "I did that for Lucas, so he'd know. But Justin…" She gulped back a surge of emotion. "He never even knew I was pregnant. I was going to tell him when he came home for my birthday."

"So you were never married. Not even secretly."

"No. You needn't worry on that account, Jordan. I have no claim on your family's precious money or anything else. So go away and leave us alone."

She studied his face for some sign that her words had made an impact. But his expression could have been chiseled in basalt.

"You might have told us," he said. "It would've meant a lot to my parents, knowing Justin had left a child."

"Your parents hated me! How could I expose my innocent baby to those ugly feelings?"

"I want to see the boy."

No! Angie's heart slammed. She'd had no warning, no time to prepare Lucas for this.

"I don't think—" she began. But it was too late. She heard the opening of the bedroom door and the cautious tread of small sneakers. Evidently Lucas had grown tired of waiting and decided to check things out for himself.

Short of lunging for her son, there was little Angie could do. She watched in mute horror as Lucas emerged from the hallway and caught sight of their visitor.

His brown eyes opened wide. Then his face lit with joyous wonder. "Daddy!" he cried, racing across the room. "Daddy, you came back!"

Daddy?

It was the last thing Jordan had expected—this pint-size bundle of energy hurtling toward him, flinging eager arms around his knees. A sense of helplessness crept over him. Lord, did the boy think he was Justin?

He lifted his gaze to meet Angie's. She looked as if she'd been punched hard enough to break a rib. With visible effort she found her voice. "He has Justin's picture. I've told him that his daddy's in heaven, but he's so young…" The words trailed off. Her eyes pleaded for Jordan's understanding.

With a firm hand, Jordan peeled the boy off his legs and boosted him onto the edge of the coffee table. The investigator had included some pictures in his packet, but they'd all been from a distance, at skewed angles as the photographer tried to avoid attention and stay out of sight. This was his first good, clear look at the boy.

If he'd had any doubts the child was Justin's, they vanished at once. Lucas had his mother's vivid *Latina* coloring, but aside from that he was all Cooper. The straight nose, the dimpled chin and unruly cowlick at the crown of the head mirrored Justin's features—and Jordan's.

Identical twins were genetic copies of each other. This boy could be his own son.

Lucas regarded him with adoring eyes, but his lower lip quivered, as if he sensed something was wrong. Maybe he was wondering why his long lost father wasn't happier to see him.

Jordan suppressed the urge to jump up and leave. He'd never spent much time around children, didn't understand them or even like them much, truth be told. But the situation called for some kind of response. He cleared his throat.

"Listen to me, Lucas. I'm not your father. I'm your uncle Jordan, your father's brother. We look alike, that's all. Do you understand?"

A single tear welled, then trickled down Lucas's cheek. Jordan glanced toward Angie. Pain was etched on her lovely, sensual face. From the moment he'd met her, he'd found himself wondering how it would feel to kiss those lush, moist lips. Then he'd found out…to his everlasting regret.

"Come here, Lucas." Angie gathered her son close. Clasping him fiercely, she glared at Jordan over the boy's head. "You still haven't told me why you're here," she said in a glacial voice.

Jordan exhaled. Where to start? He'd rehearsed his speech in the car. The words he'd chosen struck him as stuffy and arrogant now, but nothing better came to mind.

"I have a duty to my brother," he said. "Justin would want his son to have all the advantages money can buy—a home to be proud of, a quality education, social and cultural opportunities—advantages you can't afford to give him."

She pulled her son closer. "I can give him love. And when my business picks up I'll be able to give him other things, too. If you think I'd accept one cent of your money—"

"Money isn't what I had in mind, Angie."

Her eyes flashed in unmistakable horror. Did she think he was plotting to take the boy away from her? Picking up on his mother's distress, Lucas whimpered.

"Hear me out," Jordan said. "I'm inviting you and Lucas—*both* of you—to come and live at the ranch. There's plenty of room in the house. You could have as much privacy and independence as you need. You could even continue with your web design business, if you choose to. As for Lucas—"

"Stop right there! It's out of the question." Angie had gone rigid. Lucas squirmed in her arms, looking as if he were about to cry.

"I said, hear me out. When I'm finished you can make up your mind."

With a sigh she boosted Lucas off her lap. "Go back in your room and play," she said. "If you're good, we'll make popcorn and watch cartoons tonight."

As the boy scampered away, she turned back to face Jordan. "What were you thinking when you came up with this idea?" she demanded. "Your mother would barely speak to me when Justin was alive. Having me in the house now, even with Lucas, would be miserable for her—and for us."

Jordan shook his head. "Two years ago, after my father died, my mother moved to a retirement condo in town. She says she'll never go back to the ranch. Too many memories."

"So you're there alone?"

Jordan wondered if she was thinking the same thing he was. The two of them alone together in the house at night with Lucas asleep.... He squelched the idea before his imagination could seize on it and run off to forbidden places. He had every reason to despise this woman. But that didn't mean he wouldn't relish having her in his bed. Not that that would ever happen. She hated him for that single, amazing, train wreck of a kiss just as much as he hated himself.

"The ranch is never lonely," he said. "You'd be there with the housekeeping staff and the stock hands, and of course, you'd have a car. You'd be free to come and go as you like."

She glanced down at her hands. In the awkward silence, he read her unspoken question.

"You wouldn't see that much of me," he volunteered. "I spend three or four days a week at my office in town. And I do a lot of traveling. Even when I'm home, I don't wander around looking for company."

The only sign she'd heard him was the rise of color in her cheeks. He knew what she must be thinking. Hell, he'd been thinking the same thing from the moment he saw her.

He took a slow breath. "Let me make this clear. If it's me you're worried about, know that I won't lay an improper hand on you or do anything to make you feel uncomfortable. All I want is what's best for my brother's son."

Her head came up. "If you want what's best for him, you'll go away and leave us alone."

Jordan squelched the impulse to reach out and seize her shoulders. "Blast it, woman, look around you. In this neighborhood, your boy can't even go outside to play. Think of the life he could have on the ranch—open spaces, animals, caring people to look after him—"

"No!" She flung the word at him. "I'm not going to sit here and let you tell me that I'm not capable of raising my son on my own, with my own resources. This apartment may not be the lap of luxury, but we're doing just fine here without the help of you or anyone else. Listen to me, Jordan. My parents were migrant farm laborers. They worked in the fields from sunup to dark so their children could have a better life. Sometimes we slept on the ground. Sometimes we barely had enough to eat. But the one thing we never did was accept charity. And I'm not accepting your charity now."

Jordan's impatience surged. What was wrong with the woman? Didn't she understand that what he was offering wasn't a handout? The ranch was Lucas's birthright, and he had just as much right to it as Jordan did. "This isn't charity," he snapped. "Lucas is my brother's son. He's entitled to—"

"He's entitled to learn the value of hard work and have the satisfaction of earning his way in the world. I can give him that much, at least." She rose, trembling. "So take your offer and go. We don't need your help. We don't want it."

Jordan stood, looming over her. Angie's head barely came to his chin, but she looked capable of drawing blood. Time to retreat and regroup.

Scowling down at her, he nodded. "All right, I've made the decent gesture. Because you won't accept my help, all I can do is leave. But if you change your mind—"

"I won't. Goodbye, Jordan."

Without another word he strode out the door and closed it behind him. Heading down the hall, he heard the rattle of the chain latch and the click of the closing dead bolt.

What a proud little thing she was. Jordan couldn't help but admire her spirit. But in rejecting his offer, she'd made a foolish decision. She didn't deserve another chance.

But Justin's son deserved every chance, and giving him that chance was Jordan's responsibility. He remembered the joy on Lucas's face when he thought his father had returned. Now that he'd seen the boy, Jordan knew he couldn't just turn his back and walk away. Maybe he couldn't force Angie to accept his offer. But he *could* make sure she had a way to reach him in case she changed her mind.

With a sigh, he fished a business card out of his wallet and scrawled his private number on the back. Turning around, he slipped the card under the door. Angie would probably tear it up. But that was a chance he'd have to take. There was more at stake here than a woman's pride—far more than Angelina Montoya could ever know.

Two

Angie lay in a tangle of sheets and blankets, her eyes staring up into the darkness. Through the cheap plastic blinds, floodlights cast dingy streaks on the far wall. Out on the street, a motorcycle coughed, roared and faded into the night.

Jordan's card lay on the nightstand. She should've torn it to pieces or, better yet, burned it. She'd have no need to contact him because she had no intention of accepting his offer. She and Lucas were doing all right. They had a roof over their heads, enough to eat, enough to wear and enough spare change to put a few gallons of gas in the '96 Toyota she drove as little as possible.

But uncertainties dogged her every waking hour. What if her business failed? She'd be lucky to find a job that would pay enough for decent day care. What if she got sick or, worse, what if Lucas did? She could barely afford baby aspirin, let alone medical insurance. What about the years ahead? Could she pay for sports, trips and music lessons? Could she pay for college?

And how would Lucas feel when he found out his father's family was wealthy, and she'd raised him in poverty rather than take their help?

Today she'd received an offer that could end those worries. Her pride was only part of the reason she'd shown Jordan the door. To give her son a better life, she would have been willing to humble that pride. Maybe if the offer had come from Jordan's mother, she would have taken it, ignoring the way it would have burned to accept anything from a woman who'd treated her like she was no better than dirt.

So why had she really turned Jordan down?

As if she didn't know.

The memory of that fateful New Year's Eve opened in her mind like a big-screen movie. An old schoolmate of the twins had thrown a party at her home. Angie and Justin had driven there together. Jordan had come later, alone.

By the time Jordan arrived, Justin had downed enough liquor to put himself in a party mood. Their recently divorced hostess had been paying him far too much attention. Worse, Justin hadn't seemed to mind the woman's advances. After discovering the two of them in the kitchen, locked in a sloppy clinch, Angie had had enough.

Stalking toward the front door, she'd passed Jordan in the entry. Despite their past animosity, he'd appeared like a rescue beacon in a storm. Driven by desperation, she'd asked him to drive her home.

Jordan had found her coat and guided her outside to his waiting Mercedes. The night had been cold, she remembered, but the car was still warm. As she buckled herself into the cushiony leather seat, Angie had felt herself falling apart.

That very morning, in her bathroom, she'd stared in disbelief as the plus sign materialized on her home pregnancy test. She'd spent the rest of the day in shock, wondering when and how to tell Justin. Now what was she going to do?

As the motor purred to life, she'd wiped away a furious tear.

Jordan passed her a tissue box from under the dash. She hadn't told him what was wrong, but it appeared he'd drawn his own conclusion. "Sorry," he'd muttered, pulling the car onto the street. "I love my brother but when he gets a few drinks under his belt, he can be a real jackass."

Angie had huddled in silence, sniffling into the tissues he'd given her. She'd heard that pregnancy made women more emotional. Now she believed it. By the time the Mercedes pulled up to the curb in front of her apartment, she was blubbering like a fool.

Jordan had switched off the key and turned toward her. "Will you be all right, Angie?" His voice was surprisingly gentle.

She'd raised her face to the light, revealing swollen eyes and drizzly streams of mascara down her cheeks. Her throat jerked. Her lips moved in a wordless effort to speak.

He'd mouthed something that might have been a curse. Then, suddenly she was in his arms, sobbing against the shoulder of his leather coat.

He'd held her lightly at first, his lips skimming her hair as he muttered half voiced words of consolation. The manly aroma of his skin, like sagebrush after a rain, surrounded her with an aura of warmth and safety. His arms were strong, his breath a comforting murmur against her ear. She had no reason to like Jordan Cooper. But tonight she needed him.

She needed him in ways she couldn't have imagined an hour earlier.

Had it been because her hormones were out of control? Angie wondered, thinking back. Had it been because Justin had hurt her, or because her emotional state had awakened some long-buried urge? She would never know. But even now, she couldn't deny that she was as much to blame as Jordan for what happened next.

Her face had tilted upward, lips parting expectantly. It had seemed natural that he should kiss her. But she hadn't anticipated the hungry heat that exploded in the core of her body to race like wildfire through her veins.

A growl of surprise escaped his throat as he felt her response. As the kiss deepened, his arms tightened around her. Whimpering, she caught the back of his head, pulling him down to her. Her fingers raked his thick hair. Her mouth opened to welcome his probing tongue.

His hand had found its way inside her coat. Through the thin silk of her dress, his caresses triggered whorls of exquisite sensation. Angie moaned as his palm cupped her breast. She was spiraling out of control, drunk with wanting more, wanting him. As his fingertip traced a line beneath the hem of her short skirt, her thighs had parted in open invitation…

But something wasn't right, an inner voice shrilled. This man had never even pretended to be her friend. Scheming, opportunistic Jordan would stop at nothing to break his brother's engagement.

Suddenly it had all made sense. Jordan meant to sleep with her, tell Justin about it, then celebrate his victory as Justin dumped her and walked away.

And she was playing right into his hands.

"No!" She'd twisted away from him. Her palm had struck his face in a wrenching slap. Calling him the worst names she could think of, she'd scrambled out of the car. Jordan had made no move to stop her as she fled up the walk.

The following morning Justin had appeared at her door with flowers and apologies. Even after they'd made up, Angie had been hesitant to tell him about her pregnancy. And she'd never told him what had happened in Jordan's car.

The next time she'd seen Jordan was on her birthday, when he'd come to tell her Justin was dead.

Turning over, Angie punched air into her flattened pillow. She'd never known Jordan Cooper not to have an agenda. And there was no reason to doubt he had one now.

What did he want? Not her. Not sex. An attractive, powerful man like Jordan would have no trouble getting women. The issue was more likely control—legal and financial control over his brother's son and maybe over her, as well. Whatever Jordan's game, she'd be a fool to play along. When it came to pulling strings, the man was way out of her league.

Bottom line—she didn't trust him.

And she wasn't sure she trusted herself, either.

From the parking lot, curses and the sound of running feet broke into her thoughts. A gunshot rang out, followed by two more. One bullet chunked into a panel below the window. Another cracked through the glass and chipped the door frame on the far side of the room.

"Mama, I'm scared." Lucas stood in the bedroom doorway, clutching his teddy bear. The bullet had almost hit him.

"Get down! Now!" Angie dived out of bed and pulled

her son to the floor. Heart pounding, she lay on the rug, protecting him with her body as another shot shattered the window and slammed into the mattress. An eternity seemed to pass before she heard sirens wailing down the street. Gang fights happened in this part of town, but she'd never known one to come this close.

Lucas had begun to sob. "The police are on their way, Lucas," Angie whispered. "Lie still. We'll be safe soon."

And they *would* be safe, she vowed. She would get her precious son out of this neighborhood and give him a decent life—even if it meant making a deal with the devil.

Inching forward, she switched on the bedside lamp, found Jordan's card and fumbled for the phone.

Angie stood on the balcony, gazing down into the courtyard of the rambling Cooper home. The last rays of sunset cast an amber glow over hundred-year-old adobe walls. The tinkle of an ancient stone fountain blended with the distant call of a desert quail.

She'd been here before. But with the sadness of losing Justin coloring her memories, she'd forgotten how enchanting this place was. Justin had told her about the time, money and love his mother had lavished on refurbishing the historic *hacienda*. Everything here was perfect, from the stately, exposed *vigas* that supported the roofs to the Chimayo rugs, the priceless Pueblo pottery and the two Georgia O'Keefe paintings that flanked the great stone fireplace.

Now Jordan lived here by himself. Was he aware of the beauty around him, Angie wondered, or only of its value? What, exactly, made Jordan Cooper tick?

Last night, when she'd phoned him, he'd answered at once; but his manner had been so brusque that she'd suspected he wasn't alone. At first light, a pickup had arrived with two men from the ranch. They'd boxed up Lucas's toys, Angie's computer and their other personal things and had them on the road in less than an hour. Angie, with Lucas in her car, had followed the truck to Santa Fe and from there to the ranch.

Marta, the graying housekeeper, had fed them cheese *quesadillas* and shown them to their rooms on the second floor of the newer guest wing, where their boxes were waiting. The woman had been coldly polite, which puzzled Angie until she remembered that Marta had watched the twins grow up. Justin had been her special pet.

It wasn't going to be easy living in this house where people viewed her as the enemy. But Lucas seemed happy to be here. She owed it to her son to make this work.

Jordan had yet to show his face. He'd promised to leave her alone, but a word of welcome would have been reassuring. Now, as the twilight deepened around her, Angie couldn't help feeling like a stranger, unwelcome and unwanted.

Jordan paused in the shadowed doorway, studying Angie where she stood against the wrought-iron balustrade. She wore a simple turquoise sheath with flat-soled shoes. A white cardigan wrapped her against the evening chill.

For a moment Jordan found himself wishing he could erase the past, stride forward and meet her for the first time. But that was fantasy. Reality was Justin's absence and Justin's child—and the misstep that had changed everything.

Stepping into the light, he cleared his throat. "So here you are. Dinner's on the table. Where's Lucas?"

"Lucas had a bowl of cereal and went to sleep an hour ago. It's been a long day for him."

"Is he all right with the move?"

Her laugh sounded strained. "As far as Lucas is concerned, this place might as well be Disneyland. I've never seen him so excited."

"And how about you?" As she fell into step beside him, Jordan checked the impulse to brush a hand across the small of her back.

"This isn't about me. I'm here for my son."

"I didn't bring you here to punish you, Angie. What do you need?"

"Time, maybe. It's not your job to make me happy, Jordan. I'm a big girl. I can work things out for myself."

They'd reached the stone steps that descended to the patio. As she moved ahead, her perfume drifted up to him—a light floral fragrance with a sexy undertone that slammed into his senses, spinning him back in time.

He'd only meant to comfort her that night in his car. But before he knew it the situation had grown too hot to handle. By the time his fingers brushed Angie's bare thigh, Jordan's manly urges had taken over. Hang the consequences, he'd wanted her.

Angie's blistering slap had brought him back to his senses. He'd deserved her rebuke that night, and he'd done his best to accept it as a lesson learned.

But the sweet, hot feel of her had burned into his memory—and into his conscience. Now the damage was done, and there could be no going back.

"I need to apologize for waking you up last night," she said. "I'd have waited till morning, but after that scare—"

"No, you did the right thing. And you didn't wake me up. I was just…busy."

"Oh." There was a world of knowing in that single syllable.

"I'd have shown up this morning to help you move,

but I had some important business in town. I only just got home."

"Business." She shook her head. "Justin always said your business was the great love of your life. He claimed that sometimes it was all he could do to drag you away from your desk to spend time with him and your parents."

They'd entered the older, central part of the house. The living room had been left dark, but lamplight glowed through the open door of the dining room on the far side.

"There's more than one way to see to family." Jordan said. "If it weren't for my investment business, we'd be selling off parcels of land to keep this place solvent. Picture ugly housing tracts in all directions." He paused, dismissing the subject. "Are you hungry?"

"Starved."

Jordan's smile was forced. Just being with Angie ripped open old wounds, probably as much for her as for him. They were both playacting tonight, making believe the past didn't exist. But how long could they keep up the pretense before the masks fell away?

The hand-hewn table was medieval in size, a relic of the days when the ranch had entertained flocks of guests. Tonight Angie and Jordan sat alone at the end nearest the kitchen, eating chicken and sausage paella with crisp green salad and red wine. Carlos, Marta's shy young nephew who'd served the meal, had been friendly. But, then, he hadn't been here four years ago, Angie reminded herself. Odds were he and Justin would never have met.

Her gaze shifted to her dining partner. She'd never had a problem telling Justin and Jordan apart, mostly because of how they'd behaved toward her. But tonight, with Jordan making an effort to be pleasant, the resemblance was uncanny. Except for the awkwardness that hung between them, it could've been Justin sitting across from her, smiling and making small talk.

"My calendar's clear for tomorrow," he said. "I was thinking Lucas would like to see more of the ranch—with you along, of course."

Hadn't he resolved to keep his distance? Angie squelched the urge to argue. Lucas, she knew, would love an outing. "What a coincidence. My calendar's clear, too," she said.

"I know you've ridden a little. We can take horses up to the springs for a picnic. You'll want to hold Lucas on your lap, but I've got a gentle old mare that'll be fine with that."

"Sounds good." It was like Jordan, she thought, to plan the day and assume she'd just go along. Justin would've come up with the idea, then left her to carry out the details.

The silence had grown awkward. Angie scrambled for a new subject. "I'm surprised you aren't married by now, Jordan," she said.

"I was. Three years ago. Needless to say, it didn't work out."

"May I ask what happened?"

"About what you'd expect. She wanted a social life. I was always working. I wanted a family. She wanted fun. Somebody else came along." He took a sip of Cabernet. "Can't say I blame her for what happened. After eight months we were both ready to pull the plug."

"You wanted a family?" Somehow that surprised her.

"After Justin's loss, I felt I owed it to my parents to continue the Cooper line. But it was a bad idea. I don't have the patience to be a decent husband, let alone a decent father."

Angie had gone cold beneath her sweater. Was this

why Jordan had brought Lucas here—to serve as the ready-made family heir?

It was a monstrous burden to place on a small boy. But then, she should've guessed what Jordan had in mind. He wasn't thinking of Lucas. He was looking for a convenient way to discharge his family duty.

What would that mean for her? Was Jordan planning to ease her out of the picture? What if she chose to leave? What if she met someone and wanted to get married? Would Jordan fight her to keep his brother's son?

Her first impulse was to confront him. But a blowup on her first night here wouldn't be wise. She would bide her time, Angie resolved. She would watch and be wary. Any decision she made would be in the best interest of her son.

Even if it meant taking him away from this place.

She stared down at her half-finished plate, her appetite gone. "I should get back to Lucas," she said, standing. "He might wake up and be frightened."

"I'll walk with you." Jordan had risen, too.

"No, it's all right. Finish your dinner." She spun away from the table and plunged into the shadowed living room. With her eyes unaccustomed to the darkness, she could just make out the stairs. She headed straight for them.

"Angie! Wait—!"

Something crashed to the tiles as she stumbled against a side table. Her first frantic thought was that whatever she'd broken had to be expensive. As far as she knew, Meredith Cooper had never paid less than eight hundred dollars for a piece of pottery.

Her second thought was that she'd hurt herself. A sharp throbbing came from just above her knee, where she'd struck the edge of the table. Clutching the spot, she crumpled onto a nearby footstool.

"Are you all right?" Jordan's face emerged from the darkness. He crouched beside her.

"I'll pay for what I broke," she muttered between clenched teeth. "No matter how much it cost or how long it takes...."

"The damned thing's insured. Don't worry about it. Let's have a look at you."

Switching on a table lamp, he lifted her hand away from the injury. As his fingertips explored the rising lump, their touch sent shimmers of heat up her thighs. She was acutely aware of his nearness, the scent of his hair, the sound of his breathing. A moist ache stirred in the depths of her body.

"You've got a nasty bruise," he said. "We keep an ice bag in the kitchen. Hang on. I'll fill it for you."

"Please don't bother. I'll be fine." Her heart was pounding. She needed to get away.

"No bother. It'll only take a minute." Rising, he strode back through the dining room and through the swinging door into the kitchen.

Angie waited until the door had closed behind him. Then she pushed to her feet, limped out to the patio and fled up the outside stairs.

Lucas was asleep in his father's childhood bed, his hair a dark spill on the pillow. Aching with tenderness, Angie gazed down at him. Her son was so precious, so innocent and trusting, and she was all the protection he had.

All she wanted was what was best for him. But how could she know what that was? Was he safer in this place with no gangs, no sirens, no gunshots in the night...or would he be better off far away from the cool, calculating man downstairs whose agenda hadn't yet come to light?

The boxes from Lucas's old room were piled next to the bed. Angie had unpacked his clothes but left his toys, books and other small possessions for tomorrow. Now she found herself rummaging through the cardboard cartons, her fingers seeking then finding the familiar shape, the oval frame surrounding a childproof Plexiglas surface.

The moon gleamed through the window, casting its soft light on Justin's photograph. Angie's finger brushed the corner of the smiling mouth. *This* man was Lucas's father, not the gruff, scheming imposter who masqueraded behind the same face. She would remember that truth in the days ahead, and she would make sure Lucas remembered it, too.

Setting the photo on the nightstand, she turned it toward the bed, where the boy would see it when he awakened. Then, with a last glance at her sleeping son, she tiptoed out of the room.

Three

Jordan was at the kitchen table, drinking his early morning coffee, when a rumpled elf appeared in the doorway. Lucas's cowlick was standing straight up. His blue-striped T-shirt was inside out and his sneakers trailed untied laces.

He stared at Jordan for a thoughtful moment. "Are you *really* not my daddy?" he asked.

"I'm really not your daddy." Jordan tried to ignore the unaccustomed tug at his emotions. "I'm your uncle Jordan, and that's what you can call me." He looked the boy up and down. "I take it you dressed yourself. Where's your mother?"

"Mommy's asleep." His wide dark eyes, so like Angie's, roamed the kitchen. "I'm hungry. What's to eat?"

Jordan rose. Most days, coffee was all the breakfast he wanted. Marta wouldn't be here till after eight, and it

was barely seven. He could hardly let a child go hungry
that long. "What do you like?" he asked.

"Pancakes."

"All right, I'll see what I can do." There was a box of
pancake mix in the cupboard. Gathering dishes and uten-
sils, Jordan set to work. The first three pancakes stuck to
the griddle and ended up in the trash. On the next try he
had better luck. He was able to drop three respectable-
looking pancakes onto Lucas's plate.

The boy stared at the pancakes and shook his head.

"Now what's the matter?" Jordan demanded.

"Mommy makes pancakes like a teddy bear. I want
a teddy bear."

Blast it, where was the boy's mother? Jordan sighed.
"So how do I make a teddy bear?"

"Like this." Lucas arranged the pancakes to form a
head and ears. "But the head is bigger and they're all
stuck together."

"Can't believe I'm doing this," Jordan muttered as he
spooned batter onto the hot griddle. With careful turning he just managed to get his creation off in one piece.
"How's this?" he asked as he eased it onto the plate.

"Not as good as Mommy's. But you'll do better next
time."

Jordan turned off the stove, added butter and syrup
to the lopsided teddy bear pancake and poured a glass of
milk. Then he sat down to finish his lukewarm coffee.
Lucas was digging into his pancake like a little trooper.

Justin's son.

Jordan sensed impending chaos. He was just beginning
to realize how a child—and that child's mother—would
affect his well-ordered life. Having them here wouldn't
be easy. But if anything could be done to repay the terrible debt he owed his family...

"Lucas Montoya! I've been looking all over for you!" Angie stood in the doorway, hastily dressed in jeans and a pink T-shirt. Her feet were bare, her hair tousled, her face a thundercloud.

Two thoughts flashed through Jordan's mind. The first was that, even early in the morning, Angelina Montoya was one sexy woman. He could get used to seeing her like that—uncombed and sleepy-eyed, her feet bare and her shirt clinging to her trim little body. The second thought, more sobering, was that she hadn't given Lucas his father's name. Sooner or later, whether she liked it or not, that would have to be remedied.

"Uncle Jordan made me a teddy bear pancake." Lucas flashed her a syrupy grin.

"Oh?" She frowned. "You didn't have to do that, Jordan. I've made my son's breakfast every day of his life. There's no reason that should change."

She was glaring at him as if he'd tried to kidnap the boy. Jordan got the message. The battle lines had been drawn. "I was here and he was hungry," Jordan said. "Sit down and I'll make you some pancakes, too. Do you want teddy bear or regular? I do both."

"Just coffee. I'll get my own."

"Cups are on the second shelf. Help yourself." Jordan willed himself to be annoyingly cheerful. "Did you tell Lucas we were going out for a ride this morning?"

"A ride? On horses? Like cowboys?" Lucas was all eyes and ears.

"Maybe." Angie sat down at the table and swirled cream into her coffee. A bewitching spark danced in her mahogany eyes. "First show me how fast you can finish your breakfast, get cleaned up and make your bed. Then we'll see. OK?"

"OK! I'll be lightning fast, you'll see!" He cleaned

his plate and dashed for the door. Picking up her coffee, Angie strode after him.

Jordan followed her with his eyes. Angie was a good mother—loving, firm and protective. She'd done a fine job of raising Lucas on her own. But the boy was a Cooper. Justin would want him to have everything this ranch, and the Cooper money, could provide for him.

Jordan was just beginning to realize what he'd taken on. This wasn't a short-term arrangement. Justin's son wouldn't be of age for another fifteen years. As things stood now, Angie had full legal custody of the boy. She could leave tomorrow and take him anywhere she chose. She could even meet someone, marry and allow her new husband to adopt Lucas.

Jordan knew he couldn't let that happen.

It would take good lawyer to help secure Lucas's place in the family. The legal process was bound to take time, especially if Angie chose to fight him at every turn. For now, it would be up to him to make damned sure the woman was happy enough to stay put.

He couldn't bring Justin back or undo the tragic events he'd helped set in motion. But restoring his brother's son in the Cooper family might, at least, grant him a measure of redemption.

By nine o'clock they were on the trail. The docile bay Jordan had chosen for Angie moseyed along at a plodding gait. Lucas, sitting astride her lap, giggled with delight. What could be more exciting than a ride on a real horse?

The well-worn path wound through piñon-covered hills to descend into a broad arroyo where spikes of yucca and clumps of blooming chamisa rose against adobe-colored ledges. Some distance ahead, Angie knew, the way

would narrow, ending where a waterfall cascaded down
the canyon wall.

The last time she'd ridden this trail, it had been with
Justin. They'd taken a picnic to the waterfall and made
love at sunset on the blanket they'd brought. Now it was
Jordan who rode beside her on the splendid palomino she
recognized as Justin's former favorite.

Her bruised knee twinged as she shifted in the saddle.
Her face flamed at the memory of last night—Jordan's
hand gliding up her leg. In the embarrassment of the moment, she hadn't really noticed just how intimate it had
been, letting him touch her like that. Remembering it
now, the intensity of her response shocked her. She tried
to tell herself it was because he looked so much like Justin. But that didn't explain it. Justin was gone, and behind
that well-loved face was a very different man.

Today, dressed in faded denims, a western-style shirt
and a weathered Stetson, Jordan looked more at ease than
Angie had ever seen him. He sat a horse as if he'd begun
riding at Lucas's age, which he probably had.

They said little, depending on Lucas's chatter to fill
the awkward silence. He talked mostly to Jordan, asking childish questions that Jordan answered with surprising patience.

"Are you a real cowboy, Uncle Jordan?"

"I just play at being a cowboy. But there are some real
cowboys on the ranch. They work here, taking care of
the cows and horses."

"Can I be a cowboy, too?"

"Maybe not a real one. But you can play at it, like I do."

"Can I have a horse?"

"Lucas," Angie warned, "you mustn't ask Uncle Jordan to give you things."

Jordan's gaze narrowed. "Before you get a horse you'll

have to be big enough to take care of it. That's going to take some time. But you might be old enough for a puppy."

"A puppy!" Lucas squirmed with excitement.

"Only if your mother says it's all right, of course."

"We'll talk about it later." Angie gave Jordan an annoyed glance. It wasn't that she'd mind having a puppy around. Lucas would love a dog. But why couldn't the man have asked her first?

She needed to have some serious words with him. Just because she'd agreed to move out to the ranch, that didn't mean that she was going to let Jordan take over her life, or Lucas's. He had no right to make decisions about her son's care.

For the sake of Lucas's safety, she'd live under the same roof with the man. She'd even force herself to be civil. But she wasn't going to let herself fall for the "concerned uncle" act. She'd continue to monitor every conversation with him with a healthy dose of suspicion.

It didn't matter that four years had passed. Jordan still had his own agenda. And she could never trust him to be on her side.

Angie's chance to bring up the puppy came after lunch. They'd spread a blanket on the grass at the base of the waterfall, where they'd feasted on Marta's cheese *empanadas* and piñon nut cookies. Lucas's presence had kept their conversation on neutral ground, but now he was curled on the blanket, fast asleep in the warm sunlight.

"Looks like we could be here awhile." Jordan leaned back against a boulder and crossed his long, booted legs at the ankle.

"I'm afraid so." Angie felt strangely tongue-tied. "Wake him now and he'll be as cranky as a little bear."

"We can't have that, can we?" His slow grin was so like Justin's that Angie felt a lump rise in her throat.

"About that puppy," she said.

His only response was the subtle twitch of one eyebrow.

"You should know better, Jordan." She spoke in an impassioned whisper. "Getting Lucas's hopes up before you've cleared it with me—it's unfair. Worse, it's underhanded. If I say no, I'll be the villain."

His expression didn't change. "Why say no? The boy could use a playmate. A dog would be good for him."

"Maybe. But that's not your decision to make. I'm his mother. I'll decide when he's ready for a pet."

"He's my brother's son." Jordan's eyes had gone hard. "Shouldn't I have something to say about that, too?"

"Your brother's son!" It was all Angie could do to keep from raising her voice and waking Lucas. "You've known him for less than a week. How could you possibly know what would be good for him? Were you there when he was born? Did you change him and feed him and walk the floor when he cried all night?" A surge of emotion cracked her voice. She gulped back tears.

"Angie, all I did was suggest we get him a puppy."

"And now he's got his hopes up. You should've asked me first. I'd have told you to wait."

"Why wait? A pup would help him settle in."

Angie glanced down at her sleeping son. "So far, he's settling in fine. But what if we don't stay? Do you have any idea how hard it is to rent with a dog? If we had to leave the poor thing behind, Lucas would be heartbroken."

"Why wouldn't you stay?" He sat upright, leaning toward her. Angie's pulse slammed as his steely eyes locked with hers. "I've told you to consider this your home—yours and Lucas's."

Angie felt the jaws of a velvet-cloaked trap closing around her. She shook her head. "It may sound selfish, Jordan, but I can't give up my whole life to raise Lucas here—and if opportunities lead me elsewhere, then I won't be leaving alone. I certainly won't give up my son."

"But there's no reason why you'd have to go away to find opportunities. Nobody said you had to give up your life. You'll have a car, You can go into town, even work if you choose—and you'll get the chance to meet new friends. In fact, I'm having a party here this weekend."

"I can just imagine how I'd fit with your crowd—the poor girl from the *barrio* who got knocked up by your brother!"

Angie saw his mouth tighten. She plunged ahead before he could respond.

"And what about you? You could easily remarry and have children of your own. Then Lucas and I would be nothing but excess baggage. Your wife certainly wouldn't want us here."

"Damn it, Angie, why are you making it so hard for—"

His words broke off as Lucas stirred, whimpered and opened his eyes. "Hi, Uncle Jordan," he mumbled. "Is it time to go home?"

"Anytime you say, buddy."

He sat up. "Can I ride with you on your horse?"

Jordan glanced at Angie. "That's up to your mother."

"It's fine." Angie gathered up the picnic things so Lucas wouldn't see the aggravation on her face. Jordan could have invented a reason to say no. Instead, he'd made her the potential villain. He was good at that—putting her in a position where she couldn't refuse without sounding like a meanie.

Jordan boosted Lucas onto the front of his saddle and swung up behind him. Lucas's grin almost split his small face. Angie sighed. She was already losing the battle to protect her son from this manipulative man—a man who was sure to break his trusting young heart.

Jordan spent the afternoon doing paperwork in his office. He'd hoped to see Angie at dinner, maybe mend some fences with her. But he entered the dining room to find the table set for one.

When asked, Carlos explained that Angie was working on her computer. She'd come down earlier and taken a tray to her room for her and the boy.

The message was clear. He'd blown it this morning, offering Lucas a puppy without asking her first, then trying to justify himself. If he didn't want the woman to pack up and leave, he'd be smart to apologize—on his knees if necessary.

He considered going up to her room, then thought the better of it. Angie needed her private space where she could feel safe, even from him.

Especially from him.

What had gone wrong this morning? He'd wanted the outing to be pleasant. But Angie had been as prickly as a cactus, and he'd pretty much responded in kind. If Lucas hadn't awakened, their clash might have erupted into a full-scale blowup.

They'd been on edge all morning. But Jordan knew it hadn't really been about the dog. It had been about Justin.

The old memory flashed through his mind—Justin's fist crashing into his jaw, then the slamming of a door. Lord, if only he'd known what would happen next....

But he couldn't change the past. He could only try

to rebuild the future as best he could. That was why he needed Lucas.

Maybe he should come clean with Angie, tell her the whole story. But that would be a bad idea. If Angie knew the truth about how Justin had died, and his own part in the tragedy, she'd never speak to him again. She'd take Lucas and be gone in the time it took to pack her car.

It was after 10:00 p.m. when Angie carried the dinner tray down to the kitchen. Switching on the light above the sink, she took a moment to rinse and stack the dishes.

In darkness once more, she walked out onto the patio. A whimper escaped her lips as she lowered herself to a stone bench. She hadn't been on a horse in years and her thigh muscles screamed from the morning ride. The long day had worn her out, but before sleep she needed a few minutes to clear her head.

The old Spanish fountain tinkled in the stillness. Beyond the adobe walls, a waning moon hung above the Sangre de Cristo Mountains. The night breeze carried a hint of autumn chill. "Beautiful, isn't it?"

Jordan's voice, from the shadows behind her, kicked Angie's pulse to a gallop.

"I saw the light come on in the kitchen," he said. "Is there anything you need?"

She shook her head.

"I missed you at dinner. Especially since I'd planned to apologize for my high-handedness this morning."

An apology from the almighty Jordan Cooper? Her instincts sprang to high alert. "I was working," she said. "My clients depend on me to keep their websites updated."

"Something tells me you work too hard." His hands came to rest on her shoulders, strong thumbs slipping around to massage the knotted muscles at the back of her neck. The voice of caution whispered that Jordan never did anything without a purpose. Until she was sure what he was after, she should avoid accepting any favors from him. And that meant she should pull away. But his touch was pure heaven. She could feel the tension draining from her tired body. She closed her eyes.

"Feel good?" His hands moved lower to ease the tightness between her shoulder blades. She quivered as his fingers skimmed the fastening of her bra through her thin shirt.

"Mmm-hmm…" she purred.

"Since you're likely hurting from our morning ride, I can offer something even better. The pool's drained and covered for the season, but there's a hot tub on the other side of that wall. Be my guest."

Once again caution reared its head, reminding her of her resolve not to give in to his attempts to win her over. Yet the thought of that warm water easing her misery was like a siren's call. But better safe than sorry, Angie reminded herself. "It sounds lovely," she hedged, "but—"

"But you don't have a bathing suit? No problem. There's a dressing room close by. My mother kept robes and a basket of spare suits in there for guests. You're bound to find something that'll do for a dark night. Go on, now, you've run out of excuses. I'll get it warmed up."

This was a mistake, Angie chided herself as she rummaged through the oversize laundry basket. Every minute she spent with Jordan ripped away another layer of her defenses, leaving her raw and exposed. He was so like Justin, yet so different—and in all the wrong ways.

As for the swimsuits, most of them looked as if they'd been here since the 1940s. Here was a black bikini bottom that looked as if it might fit her. But the top was impossibly big. Never mind, she'd just wear her pink T-shirt.

Kicking off her jeans and underpants she pulled on the brief. As an afterthought, she unhooked her bra, worked it out from under her shirt and tossed it onto a bench with the rest of her clothes. Draping a white terry robe over her arm she followed the stone path around the garden wall.

Trust the Coopers not to have an ordinary hot tub. This one was built of native stone set low in the ground like a grotto. On one side, desert plants added to the natural setting. The other side was open to a sweeping view of the mountains.

By now the night air had grown chilly. A shimmering curtain of steam rose from the water's rippling surface.

Angie laid the robe on a stool and stepped down into the delicious warmth. Settling onto the lip of the underwater bench, she sank up to her shoulders and closed her eyes. *Heaven.*

Smiling blissfully, she opened her eyes. Only then did Angie realize she wasn't alone. From the far side of the hot tub, Jordan's face grinned back at her.

Four

"I didn't know this was going to be a party." Angie's voice was edgy, her manner clearly distrustful. Maybe she thought he was out to seduce her.

That hadn't been Jordan's intent. He'd only hoped to put her at ease, maybe relax her enough for a civil conversation that wouldn't end in her storming off to her room. But seeing her like this, with damp curls framing her face and that pink shirt clinging to her skin, was putting all the wrong ideas into his head. Time to defuse the tension.

"Should I have made margaritas?" he joked. "I can, you know. Just ask."

"I'll pass, thanks. This is an amazing hot tub. I don't remember it from before."

Before, meaning when she was here with Justin.

"I had it built for my mother, to help her arthritis." And his mother hadn't used it even once, Jordan recalled. She'd moved out soon after it was finished.

"How was Lucas after the ride?" Jordan changed the subject. "Did he say he enjoyed it?"

"It's all he's talked about. That and getting a puppy." She lifted dripping hands to slick back her hair, raising her breasts above the water. The outline of her nipples through the wet pink fabric sent a stab of heat to his loins. His swelling erection strained the crotch of his swim trunks.

This wasn't in the plan. He'd been attracted to Angie all along, and would have jumped at the chance to get her in his bed. But she'd been his brother's girl. Except for that single slip-up in his car, he'd done an admirable job of keeping his thoughts above his belt and his hands to himself.

Now here she was, warm, sexy and no longer Justin's girl—but still off limits. The irony of it was driving him crazy.

Jordan swore silently. Coming on to Angie would be a surefire way to convince her he couldn't be trusted. But right now she looked as delectable as a hot-fudge strawberry sundae with whipped cream. It was all he could do to keep from scooping her up and enjoying a few licks, maybe even...

Damn!

"You've won this round, Jordan." She settled back into the water, barely saving his sanity. "Lucas won't give me a moment's peace until he gets that puppy. But I'm warning you, if you ever pull anything like this again, without asking—"

"Lesson learned. We could look for a pup next week and surprise him. I'll get a list of good kennels."

"*Kennels?* With so many poor, sweet dogs waiting in shelters? Not on your life! I'll take Lucas to the pound tomorrow and let him pick his own. And I'll pay the adoption fee myself. That's the deal—or no deal."

"But wouldn't you rather get him a purebred, with papers, than some common mutt?"

"Jordan Cooper, I never would have taken you for a dog snob!"

Her mischievous glare, through the rising tendrils of steam, was so sensual that Jordan bit back a groan. He knew better than to think he could take her. But he ached to have her close enough to touch. Earlier, the smooth tautness of her muscles beneath his hands had roused his senses. Now the desire to smell her damp hair and feel the satiny warmth of her skin through her wet shirt burned away all caution.

"We never did finish that shoulder rub." His voice emerged thick and husky.

Her lips parted, but she said nothing to stop him as he moved alongside her and turned her shoulders away from him. He'd promised not to lay an ungentlemanly hand on her. But a friendly massage hardly qualified as improper, especially when the lady appeared willing.

He heard the sharp intake of her breath as his thumbs worked the tightness from the base of her neck. She was small-boned, almost fragile to the touch. But Jordan knew that beneath her softness was a core of tempered steel. Angelina Montoya was not a woman to be trifled with. He'd do well to remember that—now and in the days ahead.

Angie stifled a moan as his skilled fingers moved downward. What had begun as a chaste massage in the patio garden was evolving into something warm and sensual.

In the four years since Justin's death, she hadn't even

dated. At first she'd been grieving. Then she'd been too busy rebuilding her life, earning a living and caring for her son. Strange, she'd almost forgotten how it felt to be touched by a man.

Delicate nerve endings quivered under the pressure of Jordan's strong thumbs, shooting spirals of heat down her limbs and into the root of her belly. Slumbering urges woke and trembled. The moisture that slicked the crotch of her bikini had nothing to do with being in the water. Her control was sliding away and she had no will to stop it.

She should say something, she thought—start a conversation about something trivial that would break the tension. But her mind refused to form words, and Jordan wasn't talking, either.

Angie's head fell back as he manipulated her shoulder blades, working away the tension. Her nipples contracted like tiny fists, throbbing deliciously. How would it feel if his hands were to slide around to cradle her breasts through the clinging fabric of her T-shirt? Would he do it? Heaven help her, *did she want him to?*

His fingers had reached the hem of her shirt. Slipping them beneath, he kneaded the small of her back. His touch on her bare skin triggered a rush like water breaking through winter ice. Her pulse slammed as his hands slid up her spine.

And abruptly halted.

"Massage over." He withdrew his hands and eased away from her. She turned, staring at him in the darkness.

"I made you a promise, Angie." His voice was a growl. "I don't intend to break it, especially not on your second night here. Now off to bed for both of us. It's getting late, and I've got meetings in town tomorrow."

Hot-faced, she found the step, pushed out of the pool

and grabbed the robe she'd left nearby. Wrapping it around her dripping body, she looked back. Jordan was still in the hot tub. "Aren't you coming?" she asked.

"In a minute. Go on." He glanced down at the water. Only then did it hit her. The seemingly innocent massage had affected Jordan, too—in a way a man couldn't hide.

Knotting the robe and yanking it tight, she fled to the dressing room.

How could she have let it happen?

Angie lay awake in the darkness, her thoughts churning.

From the first time she'd met him, Jordan Cooper had been her enemy. He'd fought against her engagement to Justin, and, like the rest of his family, he almost certainly blamed her for his brother's plane crash. Rightly so, Angie reminded herself. If she'd taken the money he'd offered and broken their engagement, Justin would still be alive.

Jordan had every reason to hate her.

Now she was under his roof, and she had something he wanted—Justin's son. He was already insinuating himself into her little boy's life; and Lucas, so hungry for a father's love, was falling under his spell.

Was he working his spell on her, too?

His "friendly" shoulder rub had aroused her to the melting point before he backed off, leaving her stunned and confused. Now she realized that Jordan had known exactly what he was doing.

How could she have forgotten that New Year's Eve in his car, when his kisses had made her ache for more? He'd had an agenda then. He had one now. And that agenda was never, ever about her. She was just the tool he used to get his way. Back then, he'd wanted to drive a wedge between Angie and his brother. Now, he wanted her closer…

so that he could work his way into her son's life. As always, he was out to win, and he was weighting the odds in his favor.

With or without her help, Jordan was already making headway on his plans. Lucas loved the ranch, and he was over the moon about getting his own dog. For her to take him away and shut him into another cramped apartment would be devastating. She had to give her son this chance at a better life. But that didn't mean stepping aside and letting Jordan take over.

Tonight Jordan had been angling for her trust, reeling her in just before he remembered his so-called promise. The worst of it was she'd almost fallen for his act. For that, she had no one to blame but herself.

Jordan's touch had ignited a smoldering heat that burned through her body. His resemblance to Justin might have explained that. But deep down, Angie knew better.

Tonight in the hot tub, she hadn't been thinking about Justin at all.

Jordan pulled his Mercedes into the drive at 4:25 the next afternoon. His heart dropped when he saw that Angie's beat-up Toyota was missing. Had he pushed her too far? Had she packed up and left?

Relief dawned as he remembered she'd planned on taking Lucas to choose his puppy. Climbing out of the driver's seat, he saw her old blue sedan chugging up the road toward the house. That car would have to be replaced, he reminded himself. The tires were bald and the engine, he suspected, was on the verge of throwing a rod. Worse, it might not hold up in an accident. He wanted Angie and Lucas to be safe. He could only hope she wouldn't be as stubborn about the car as she'd been about the dog.

And speaking of the dog... Jordan braced himself as

the car pulled up on the far side of the driveway. Growing up, he and Justin had shared a beautiful golden retriever named Sunny. He'd hoped to find a similar animal for Lucas. But Angie's insistence had won out. What kind of dog would a three-year-old choose from the city pound? He was about to find out.

He kept his distance as Angie got out of the car and opened the back door to unbuckle Lucas's car seat. The boy tumbled out, gripping a red plastic leash.

"Look, Uncle Jordan!" He tugged at the leash, pulling his new pet out behind him. "His name's Rudy!"

The dog that crept out of the car was past the cute puppy stage and of no discernible breed. With a short brown-and-white coat, droopy ears and a long nose, it might have been some kind of hound mix. The size of its feet hinted that it still had a lot of growing to do.

Jordan groaned.

"Come here, Rudy!" Lucas ordered, tugging at the leash.

The dog glanced around shyly, then slunk over to its new master and wound its skinny body around Lucas's legs. It had the saddest brown eyes Jordan had ever seen.

Jordan caught Angie's gaze, his eyebrows lifting in an unspoken question.

"He was red-tagged," Angie said. "They were going to put him to sleep. Lucas saved him. Just look at that face, Jordan. If ever an animal needed love…"

Jordan sighed. The dog was no beauty, but Angie's expression was so damned appealing that he wanted to grab her in his arms and kiss her till she whimpered. That wasn't practical, so he decided on the next best thing.

"We don't know where all Rudy's been," he said to Lucas. "Before we give him the run of the place, what do you say we give him a bath? You can put him in the garage while I change my clothes and get a wash tub. You might want to change, too."

Jordan hadn't asked Angie to help bathe the dog, but when he came back out to the patio with the tin tub, a bar of soap and an old towel, she was there, wearing ragged jeans and pink rubber flip-flops. They filled the tub, adding some warm water from the kitchen. Then Angie and Lucas went to fetch the dog.

The back door to the garage opened off the patio. They returned moments later with Angie holding the leash. Rudy was clinging to his young master's legs like a barnacle, terror flashing in the whites of his chocolate eyes. Damned dog probably thought he was about to be slaughtered.

Jordan reached out to lift the dog into the tub. Rudy cringed, whimpering. Maybe he'd had a man kick him around in his former life. He might be calmer with Angie or Lucas. But Jordan wasn't about to risk their getting bitten.

"Come on, boy." Jordan got a hand under the dog's bony rump, scooped him up and lowered him into the tub. Rudy made no attempt to bite. But at the first touch of water, he thrashed like an eel and howled like an Irish banshee.

Swearing under his breath, Jordan shoved the mutt all the way into the tub. Rudy was putting up the fight of his life, yelping so piteously that Jordan half expected the Humane Society to come screaming up the drive.

"Let me help. You'd better stay back, Lucas." Angie grabbed the soap and began sudsing the dog's hide. It appeared that Rudy had never had a bath in his miserable life. He kicked and struggled, splashing soapy water in all directions. By now Jordan was wet from head to toe. Gazing at him over the squirming dog, Angie burst into giggles. Her laughter was pure enchantment, bubbling like music out of some secret place.

Justin had said he'd fallen in love the first time he heard Angie laugh.

Lucas began to giggle, too, the sound a childish echo of his mother's. Ignoring her warning, the boy pushed between them. Now they were all getting soaked. Between the wriggling mutt, the splashing water and their wet clothes, the simple task of bathing a dog had become a circus. Something stirred in Jordan's throat. Was it a chuckle? He gave in and let it go. It felt good. Damned good.

Still laughing, they managed to get Rudy rinsed and out of the tub. Lucas squealed with delight as Rudy shook water in all directions. Jordan tackled the mutt for a quick toweling. Then he put the dog in the garage with an old sleeping bag, some food and a bowl of water.

"Will Rudy be OK in there?" Lucas asked.

"He'll be fine. We'll find him his own doghouse tomorrow." Jordan recalled that Sunny's old kennel was somewhere in storage. He tossed spare towels to Lucas and Angie. "For now, what do you say we dry off and go inside for some grilled cheese sandwiches and hot cocoa?"

The idea hadn't struck him until he spoke, but it seemed like a good one. Marta was off shopping, but he was a fair hand with grilled cheese himself.

By now the sun was low in the sky. A chilly autumn breeze drifted across the patio. Inside the house, Jordan lit the fireplace and moved the leather armchairs in close. Leaving Angie and Lucas to soak up the warmth, he headed into the kitchen.

He was slicing thin squares of cheese when he heard Angie's voice behind him. "Can I help with something?"

"You can make the cocoa. Mix is in the cupboard. Milk's in the fridge." Jordan didn't really need her help, but he liked the thought of her working next to him. Damned if he hadn't enjoyed bathing the fool dog this afternoon. The gloomy old house hadn't heard so much laughter in years.

Not since Justin had died.

"What's Lucas up to?" he asked. "Will he be all right alone?"

"Lucas has dozed off. If he wakes up, he'll know his way to the kitchen." Angie measured cups of milk into a pan and turned the stove on low heat. The accidental brush of her hip against his sent a jolt of awareness through Jordan's body.

"I wanted to thank you for helping with the dog," she said. "Rudy may not look like much, but Lucas already loves him."

Jordan lay the buttered sandwiches on the griddle. "Since he's Lucas's dog, that's all that matters."

"You've been exceptionally nice this afternoon." Angie stirred the cocoa powder into the warming milk.

"Exceptionally?" His hand caught the small of her back. The spoon clattered into the pan as he swung her around to face him. "I'm not a monster, Angie. I'm doing my best to make you and Lucas feel at home here."

She made no effort to pull away. Her face was inches away from his own, her moist lips parted. The urge to taste those lips was more than Jordan could stand. His thumb caught the curve of her jaw, tilting her face upward. He could feel her racing pulse as he bent closer.

With a sharp breath, she backed away. Her face was flushed. "You're about to burn the sandwiches," she said, grabbing a spatula.

Jordan bit back an apology as she flipped the toasted

bread in the nick of time. He wasn't going to claim he was sorry for acting on something both of them wanted—and he was certainly experienced enough to know when a woman wanted to be kissed. Angie had given every sign of it. But he suspected her reason for backing off involved more than grilled cheese sandwiches.

"This has to be said, so I might as well say it now." She'd gone back to stirring the cocoa. "I know we have… a history, Jordan, most of it bad. When Justin and I were engaged, you and your parents looked down on me and did everything you could to break us up. You even offered me money to leave him. Do you have any idea how much that hurt me? I'm not going to lie and say that there isn't some chemistry here. But we can't get involved—not if you expect me to stay. There's too much baggage between us. Sooner or later it would get in the way."

"Angie, I didn't mean—"

"Let me finish. You brought me here because I'm Lucas's mother. But I'm also the person responsible for Justin's death. If I'd broken up with him, he'd still be alive. Remind yourself of that the next time you're tempted to cross the line."

The words slammed into Jordan like a shotgun blast. For the past four years Angie had carried that awful burden, blaming herself for Justin's accident. She deserved to know the full story. But how could he tell her now, when the truth would drive her away? She would almost certainly take Lucas and leave. And she would never forgive him for what he'd done.

He wanted to say that he understood, even that he shared her guilt. But telling her would only make things worse.

The awkward silence between them was broken by

Lucas, who came yawning into the kitchen. "I smell cocoa. Do you have marshmallows, Uncle Jordan?"

"Not this time, but I'll add them to the shopping list." Jordan put the sandwiches on a tray while Angie filled two mugs and a cup. They ate in front of the fireplace with darkness falling outside. A soft rain had moved in to patter against the windows.

It was nice— A little like being a family, Jordan thought. Except that he could feel the tension radiating from Angie, where she sat with Lucas nestled against her side. She'd been right, he knew. Taking up where they'd left off that night in his car would be a sure way to shatter their fragile truce and bring up the ugliness of the past. They could only move forward—as friends if they could manage it. If not, as adversaries.

But as lovers? No, it would never work. Not because he blamed her for his brother's death—but because he blamed himself.

By the time they'd finished eating, Lucas had begun to nod off again. Angie rose and lifted him in her arms. "It's early but I think he's out for the night. I'm going to put him to bed."

"You're welcome to come back," Jordan said.

She shook her head, as he'd known she would. "I've been away from my business all day and I've got lots of catching up to do."

"Don't work too late." He rose and began gathering up the mugs and saucers. Without her and the boy, the room seemed too large, too quiet. Slipping on a light rain jacket he went outside and cleaned up the debris from the dog bath. Damned if it hadn't been fun, with the mutt splashing around and the three of them laughing like crazy. He'd almost forgotten what fun—that kind of fun, at least—could be like.

That reminded him, he hadn't called Whitney in days. For the past few months, he'd had an easy sexual relationship with the pretty blond socialite—a relationship he had no plans to make permanent. She was growing more possessive of late and more demanding in her needs—she wouldn't be pleased that he'd gone nearly a week without calling. A phone call would pacify her…for now. Later, he'd figured out how to cool things down between them.

His fingers hesitated over the keys of his cell phone before he put the device back in his pocket. The call could wait until tomorrow. He'd be in town then. They could have a nice, uncomplicated lunch at *La Fonda.* She'd also be coming for his party this weekend, probably expecting to stay the night. With Angie here, that might prove awkward—another thing he'd need to deal with.

Restless, he glanced up at the second floor windows. Lucas's room was dark, but Angie's light was on. He imagined her bent over her keyboard, toiling into the night. There was no need for her to work—he'd told her that much. But he knew better than to try and stop her. Angie was a proud, independent woman, determined to earn her own way.

Years ago he'd dismissed her as a gold digger, scheming to get her hands on Justin's money. He knew better now.

Wandering back inside, he spent some time going over the ranch books in his office. By the time he finished he was tired enough for bed.

He hadn't heard so much as a whine from Rudy all evening. The mutt was probably too scared to make a peep. But it wouldn't hurt to check the garage.

Jordan stepped out onto the patio. The rain had stopped, but the night air had taken on a distinct chill. Angie's light was out. He imagined her curled in bed, her hair black silk against the pillowcase, her lips as soft as a child's in sleep. Those lips had nearly been his downfall tonight, he reminded himself. If he wanted to keep Angie here, he would have to learn to treat her like a sister.

A short breezeway connected the patio to the rear of the garage. Jordan's heart dropped as he approached the door. It stood partway open.

"Rudy?" Whistling softly, he took the flashlight from its bracket next to the door and shined it in all directions. He saw no sign of Lucas's dog.

He forced himself to think clearly. There was no way for the mutt to get out of the patio area. Rudy had to be here somewhere.

Acting on a sudden hunch, he mounted the stairs to the balcony. Lucas's room, which adjoined Angie's, had its own outside door. Tonight it wasn't locked.

Moving stealthily he opened the door. Lucas was sprawled under the covers, fast asleep. On the rug, Rudy raised an alert head. Jordan couldn't be sure, but he fancied he heard a puppyish growl.

"It's all right, boy. You keep your master safe." Jordan felt an unaccustomed tug of tenderness. He'd never been fond of children. But this innocent little boy was already staking out territory in his heart.

Before closing the door, he shined the flashlight around the room. Everything was in order—clothes put away, books on the shelf, toys piled in the toy box. As Jordan moved the light beam toward the bed, something stopped him cold.

Justin's face smiled at him from the framed photo on the nightstand.

Justin, the good brother. The beloved brother. It was

a sharp reminder that even though he was gone, Justin would always stand between Jordan and the family that could never be his.

Five

Angie had tried to argue her way out of attending Jordan's party. But he'd turned a deaf ear to her protests. She and Lucas were family, he'd insisted. Keeping them hidden away would only spark nasty rumors. The sooner people learned the truth about their presence, the sooner they'd accept the situation—and Lucas. It would be better to face them at a party, when she knew they were coming, rather than running into them by chance.

He was probably right, she conceded as she surveyed her reflection in the mirror. If she faced his friends while she was ready—dressed for the part and prepared to charm—then she could control the impression she made. Her outfit—a simple black sheath, silver hoop earrings and bright red stilettos—made her look like she belonged. She knew how to dress for a party. Still, she couldn't help feeling as if she were about to walk into a den of hungry lions. She didn't fit in with Jordan's crowd and probably never would. But for the sake of Lucas's future, she had to try.

The party was an annual pre-holiday event. Most of the guests would be business associates, Jordan had told her. But there would be personal friends among them—some who'd known Justin and even a few who'd known *her*.

Glancing out through the twilight she saw cars coming up the drive—Jaguars, Porsches, a red Maserati, a vintage Corvette and more, all reminders of her own lowly status. Maybe it wasn't too late to disappear.

Jordan tapped lightly on her open bedroom door. "Ready?"

She turned to face him. "This is a mistake, Jordan. People are going to talk."

"Let them." He walked toward her. "After the first buzz, you'll be old news. You look ravishing, by the way."

Angie ignored the compliment. "You didn't need to come up here. I'm perfectly capable of going downstairs by myself."

"And hiding in the corner?" His eyebrow quirked. "I'm not about to sweep you under the rug, Angie. You deserve better and so does Lucas."

Angie gulped back the nervous lump in her throat. "Speaking of Lucas, have you checked on him?"

"He's in the den, watching movies with Carlos and Rudy. They've got pizza, popcorn, root beer, the works. If you don't show up sooner, Carlos has instructions to tuck him into bed at nine."

"Thank you," Angie said, meaning it. One thing she and Jordan had agreed on—Lucas was not to be trotted out and put on display for the party guests. The news that Justin had left a son would cause enough buzz for now.

More than enough to stir up a beehive of wagging

tongues, Angie thought as they reached the top of the stairs. Only Jordan's firm hand at the small of her back kept her from bolting.

By now most of the guests had arrived. About forty in number, they milled in the open space of the parlor, dressed in elegant evening clothes, nibbling hors d'oeuvres and sipping cocktails. Jordan had hired a catering service for the cocktails and light buffet, sparing his small household staff, but Marta was there, watching over her kitchen. The housekeeper had warmed to Luong, but she still cast cold-eyed looks at Angie—as she'd likely be doing tonight.

Eyes swiveled upward as Angie and Jordan descended the curving staircase. The murmur of conversation died into silence. "Smile!" Jordan muttered under his breath. "You're not going to a blasted funeral."

Angie arranged her features into a confident mask. Her four-inch heels wobbled with every step. She clasped Jordan's proffered arm. Even that small gesture would raise eyebrows, but it was better than risking a tumble.

They had reached the foot of the stairs. Plucking a flute of champagne from a passing tray, Jordan pressed the stem into her hand. She took a tiny sip, resolving to remain clear-headed for the entire evening.

"Chuck, this is Angie Montoya, my late brother's fiancée." Jordan introduced her to a middle-aged stranger, one of his employees. "She and their son are staying here at the ranch."

So there it was, the unvarnished truth in two neat sentences. The bespectacled man murmured a polite greeting, appearing disinterested. Maybe Jordan had chosen him for practice.

Variations on the same theme were repeated with another half-dozen guests. Responses ranged from cold politeness to curiosity. Angie pulled Jordan aside. "I'm sure the word's gotten around by now," she whispered. "There's no need for you to hover, Jordan. Go tend to your party."

"You'll be all right?"

"Just go."

Angie stood alone next to the Georgia O'Keefe painting of white Datura blossoms. She took nervous sips of champagne, fighting the temptation to leave. That would be the coward's way out. She needed to prove that she could stand up to this snobbish crowd on her own.

Her gaze scanned the room. She recognized a few people from her time with Justin; but most of the guests were strangers. A leggy blonde, elegantly clad in green silk jersey, had attached herself to Jordan's arm. She was laughing, leaning against him as she balanced her drink in her free hand. Jordan appeared to be enjoying her company. Angie remembered the late-night call she'd made to him from her old apartment. When he'd answered his cell, she'd sensed he wasn't alone. As she made the obvious connection, something hardened the pit of her stomach.

Was it jealousy?

Ridiculous! She shook her head. Jordan wasn't her property. He'd had a life before tracking her down, and that hadn't changed. Why should it?

"Angie? My God, it's really you!" The speaker was a lanky, sandy-haired fellow who'd been a friend of Justin's. She groped for his name. Travis? No, Trevor. That was it. Trevor Wilkins.

"It's been a long time," she said guardedly.

He moved close, looming over her. "You disappeared

on us after Justin's crash. I always wondered what happened to you."

"What happened to me was my son. But if you've had your ears open tonight, you probably know that."

"I did hear something to that effect. In any case, motherhood becomes you. You're more beautiful than ever."

Good grief, was the man hitting on her? Angie edged backward against the corner of the fireplace. Trevor closed the space between them. She could smell the whiskey on his breath. Her gaze darted past his shoulder to where Jordan was standing with a cluster of his guests. He appeared to be lost in conversation, the striking blonde still draped against his side.

"You know, Angie, I always did have a thing for you," Trevor was saying. "With Justin gone and Whitney, over there, staking her claim to Jordan, I was hoping you and I…"

"What I'd really like to do is catch up with the old crowd," Angie said, grasping at any excuse. "Jordan said some of them would be here. Maybe you could walk me around the room to find them."

"Sure. They'll all be glad to see you again." He offered his arm. "Maybe later, you and I could—"

"Later I have a three-year-old to take care of. For the present, the only man in my life is my son."

As he watched Angie walk off on Trevor's arm, Jordan felt a tightening in his gut. At first she'd looked as if she needed rescuing, but Trevor had evidently won her over. She was chatting away, looking perfectly happy.

And so damned sexy he wanted to fling her over his shoulder and carry her off to his bed.

Whitney was walking her manicured fingernails up

the sleeve of his jacket in a silent demand for attention. The glamorous blonde had her charms, but her insistence on always being center stage was wearing on him. Ignoring her ploy, he tore his gaze away from Angie and forced himself to focus on what Len Hargrove, his firm's longtime attorney, was trying to tell him.

"You didn't ask me, Jordan, but my advice would be to take your time. Make sure the boy's really Justin's before you take any legal steps. For all you know, the mother could have cooked up this scheme to take advantage of your family."

"Take advantage?" Jordan had to rein himself in to keep from decking the man. "She never contacted me at all—I'm the one who tracked her down. When I did, she showed me the door. She only agreed to come here after a gang fight broke out within shooting distance of her apartment. Is that what you'd call taking advantage?"

The lawyer frowned. "I can understand your sympathy for her. But shouldn't you at least have a DNA test done?"

"To prove what I already know?"

"It never hurts to be sure."

Jordan thought of Angie and how it would wound her if he demanded proof of Lucas's paternity. "I *am* sure," he said. "Everything adds up. The boy's a Cooper. Case closed."

"What does your mother have to say about all this?"

"That remains to be seen."

Jordan felt a shadow of misgiving as he spoke. Sooner or later the issue of his mother would have to be faced. Meredith Cooper was in declining health, but she was of sound mind and still the legal head of the family. The future could hinge on her acceptance of Lucas—and Angie, whom she still blamed for Justin's death. Since Jordan had vowed to spare her the truth about that tragic night, he'd be walking a tightrope.

That was the trouble with secrets. They had a way of surfacing right when they could do the most damage.

"Jordan, be a sweetie and steer me to a margarita. I've got a powerful thirst." Whitney's throaty voice broke into his thoughts. This time Jordan welcomed her demand. He'd gotten sucked into a conversation that should've taken place behind closed doors. Next time he met Len, he'd stick to a less volatile subject.

As he guided Whitney toward the bar, he caught a glimpse of Angie. She was standing on the far side of the room chatting with a cluster of their old friends. Jordan knew she'd been nervous about meeting them again, but she seemed to be managing fine.

Trevor's hand rested possessively at the small of her back. The bastard hadn't wasted any time making his move. But that was none of his business, Jordan reminded himself. Angie was her own woman. He had no right to dictate her personal life.

Leaning close, Whitney blew an alcohol-scented breath into his ear. She'd be expecting to stay the night, of course. But he wasn't in the mood for going through the motions, which was all their relationship had amounted to lately. Freeing her to find someone else would be a kindness, Jordan told himself. But that didn't mean it would be easy. He didn't like hurting people. He'd done enough of that in the past.

Now, with Angie and Lucas here, that past was coming back to haunt him.

Angie woke with a start. After an instant's confusion, she realized she was in the den on the sofa. The lighted digits at the base of the big-screen TV showed the time—11:25 p.m.

It all came back to her now—how she'd excused herself from the party at nine-thirty and gone to make sure Carlos had put Lucas to bed as instructed. She'd found the den dark, the TV turned off and the snacks cleared away.

After a long evening in high heels, her weary feet had demanded a rest. Kicking off her red stiletto pumps, she'd curled up among the cushions. She'd planned to return to the party in a few minutes. Instead, she'd fallen sound asleep.

Gathering her shoes, she tiptoed out of the room. The party was over, the house dark and quiet. The only sign of life was a faint light from the hallway that led to the master suite, where Jordan slept.

Resolving not to disturb him, Angie crossed the darkened parlor. She had just reached the staircase when a woman's angry voice shrilled down the corridor.

"This isn't about us, Jordan. It's about *her!* I was watching you tonight! You couldn't take your eyes off that cheap piece of trash!"

Angie froze as she realized the woman was talking about her.

"Keep your voice down, Whitney." Jordan spoke in a calming tone. "Angie has nothing to do with this. I'm trying to do the right thing by my brother's son. That's all."

"Ha! I heard the way you defended her to that lawyer. I was afraid you were going to punch him. That little *chiquita* is reeling you in, just like she did your brother!"

"That's enough." Jordan's voice had dropped to a growl. "I'd advise you to go now before we say things we'll both regret."

"Fine! I'm going, and I won't be back. But you're a

blind fool, Jordan. That girl will destroy you, just like she destroyed Justin!"

With those parting words, Whitney stormed into the hall, slamming the bedroom door behind her. Angie shrank into the shadows as the blonde woman charged past her and out the front door. Seconds later the roar of an engine and the squeal of tires faded into silence.

Angie hardly knew what to think as she processed everything she'd overheard. She knew that Jordan was attracted to her—that much had been perfectly clear. But the blonde woman had implied that it went much further than that—that he cared for her, that he *defended* her, that she truly mattered to him above and beyond her role as Lucas's mother. Was it true?

Did it matter? She'd already decided that they couldn't be together. The past was too much of an obstacle to overcome. Jordan would never be able to fully forgive her for what happened to Justin. And now she'd ruined things for him with his girlfriend, too.

Stumbling in tear-blinded haste, Angie started up the stairs.

"Angie?"

She turned. Jordan was standing below her, his face pale in the reflected light from the front porch. "You heard that?"

She nodded, wishing she could shrink to ant size and crawl under the nearest rug. "I never meant to. I'd fallen asleep in the den, and I was on my way back to my room." She faked an unconvincing laugh. "Maybe we can pretend it was just a bad dream I had."

"Come down here." His voice sent a quiver through her body. Angie willed herself to move toward him. Pretending, she sensed, was no longer an option.

* * *

They stood face-to-face at the foot of the stairs. Even in the darkness Jordan could see the glimmer of tears in her eyes.

"This is all my fault," she whispered. "I should never have come here."

"None of what you heard was your fault. Whitney and I were headed for a breakup. It was just a matter of getting it over with."

"But the awful things she said—that I'd destroy you like I destroyed Justin…"

Jordan fought the impulse to crush her in his arms. "You didn't destroy Justin, Angie. You're not the one who brought down that plane."

"But I could've broken up with him. I would never have taken your money, Jordan, but I could have ended the relationship, anyway—told him that I didn't want to come between him and his family." Her voice broke. "I'd have done anything to save him!"

"You couldn't have known what would happen. Neither of us could've known." Jordan felt the cold knife of guilt twisting in his gut. They had both loved Justin. But Angie wasn't the one who'd let Justin down. For that, he had no one to blame but himself.

Angie's tears had spilled over, leaving silvery trails down her cheeks. Jordan felt a lump of pain break loose inside him. With a half-muttered curse, he gathered her close. Right now he needed her, and something told him she needed him, too.

She nestled against him like a child seeking comfort after a bad dream. Her light, musky fragrance was the one he remembered from that New Year's Eve in his car—the night that had changed everything. Bittersweet memories rushed over him as he breathed her into his senses—recalling the taste of that ripe plum mouth, her warm breasts molding to his hand, the satiny smoothness of her thigh beneath her skirt....

He'd wanted Angie Montoya from the first time he saw her with his brother. He'd wanted her that night, and, damn his soul to Hades, he wanted her now.

His sex rose and hardened as he held her. There was no way she couldn't feel it. But even though she was trembling, she didn't pull away. Her arms crept around his ribs, binding their bodies even closer. With his erection cradled against her firm belly, he couldn't help thinking of where he really wanted to be—buried to the hilt inside her.

"Jordan..." Her lush lips shaped his name. *"I need..."*

He silenced her with what began as a gentle kiss. As she pressed upward, her mouth opening in invitation, the kiss deepened. His tongue feathered the sensitive inner edge of her lips, teasing her until she moaned and stretched on tiptoe to lift her hips closer to his erection. Jordan was dimly aware of her shoes dropping to the floor as he seized her taut buttocks and hauled her upward, grinding her mound against his sex. She was gasping, almost sobbing by the time he found the zipper at the back of her dress.

That night in the car, they'd managed to stop before things got out of control. But there would be no stopping now.

The bedroom wasn't far. Angie clung to Jordan as he half carried her down the hall. Her head was spinning, her blood keening through her veins, drowning the feeble protests of common sense. How could she have forgotten what it was like—the sweet rush of sensations, the overpowering need? With every throb of her pulse, she wanted this man. Her woman's body hungered for the feel of him, the scent and taste of him.

Her dress gapped open in back where Jordan had yanked down the zipper. His fingers worked the fastening of her black lace bra, deftly parting the single clasp. The touch of his hand on her skin sent a warm shock spiraling through her body. All she could think of was *more*. Her frantic fingers tore at the front of his shirt. Buttons clattered onto the tiles as they stumbled down the hallway.

They reached the side of the king-size bed. He lowered her bare feet to the rug long enough to strip off her dress. The bra came with it, sliding down her body to pool around her ankles. She kicked the clothes aside as he flung back the covers, swept her up in his arms and all but flung her onto the sheets.

Clad in nothing but her wispy black panties, she lay watching as he ripped off his clothes to reveal a lean, muscular torso. He shoved his briefs down his hips, freeing his erection to spring up, as hard and sleek as a marble column.

Neither of them spoke. Jordan seemed to know that words would only complicate things. So did she. Angie quivered as he leaned over her. She felt a breath of hesitation—he was so experienced, so sure. Was she about to make a fool of herself? But her arms were already reaching up to pull him down to her. He groaned as he buried his face between her breasts, inhaling the scent of her skin, mouthing her nipples with a hunger that sharpened the secret longings inside her. Strange, how the notion of Jordan Cooper needing anyone hadn't entered her mind until now. But how could she not believe that he needed her as much as she needed him?

Her head fell back as he stroked her. His hands ranged downward over the flat of her belly, sliding her panties off her hips, working them downward until they were lost in the bedclothes. His palm slid back up to skim the crisp, black curls between her thighs. She whimpered, thrusting her hips to meet his touch, wanting him to caress her, to taste her.

Her hands raked his hair, urging his head downward. Sensing what she wanted, he shifted his weight and brushed a line of kisses down her belly. Her breath stopped as he settled between her legs. His breath warmed her sex. His tongue separated her folds, licking the exquisitely sensitive bud at their center. Her womb contracted like a fist. Her hands clenched and unclenched in a frenzy as he sucked her. She came within seconds, spasms of pleasure shuddering through her body. Moisture slicked her thighs. She was ready for him—aching to feel him inside her.

His deft fingers paused to add protection. Then, shifting forward, he entered her in one gliding thrust. As his length and bulk filled her she forgot to breathe, struck by the wonder of what was happening—and the irony of it. This was Jordan inside her, her longtime foe; Jordan loving her—except that it wasn't love. She had no illusions about that. He might care for her more than she'd previously suspected, but this had nothing to do with *care*. It was pure, unbridled lust.

Her thoughts dissolved as he began to move, the gliding friction of his sex awakening freshets of sensation. Her hands clawed at his back as he drove into her harder and faster. She felt herself clench around him in rhythmic spasms that exploded through her body as she met his thrusts. Her lips formed his name silently. *Jordan... Jordan...*

He groaned, burying himself deep as he climaxed. Overcome by an unexpected tenderness, Angie cradled him between her thighs, rocking him gently as they floated back to Earth.

There were no words between them. He chuckled softly, grinning down at her in the darkness. Then, brushing a kiss on her lips, he rolled to one side and fell asleep.

Six

Angie lay in the dark, listening to the sounds of Jordan sleeping beside her. The easy flow of his breathing was broken by an occasional snore. She might have found it sweetly comforting—if she hadn't just made one of the worst mistakes of her life.

She'd agreed to a platonic arrangement for Lucas's sake. But tonight, in Jordan's arms, her good intentions had melted like pine pitch in a raging bonfire.

Now what? Jordan might expect more of the same. But there was no way she could remain here as his live-in lover—especially not with Lucas. Children lost their naïveté early these days. If this became a regular thing, the boy was bound to discover that his mother was sneaking off to Uncle Jordan's bed.

Could the man be thinking of marriage for Lucas's sake? But that idea was a joke. Four years ago Jordan had come up with a plethora of reasons why Justin shouldn't wed her—her family background, her poverty, even her ambition. None of those reasons had changed. Jordan might care for her, might show protectiveness and concern, might even be willing to have an ongoing sexual relationship with her. But marriage would never be possible. The Coopers were Santa Fe royalty. They would always look down on her—and they would never forgive her part in Justin's death.

Rising onto one elbow, she studied Jordan's face. In sleep he looked nothing like the cynical, hard-driving man she knew during his waking hours. She had to struggle to remember that even now, she couldn't completely trust him. And the longer she stayed in his bed, the more tempting it would be to forget. For her own peace of mind, she had to get away from him. Right now.

Inching toward the side of the bed, she lowered her feet to the floor and fumbled for her clothes. Her panties were lost in the bed but she found her bra. Hooking the back and pulling on her rumpled dress, she tiptoed down the hall and up the stairs.

Back in her room, she opened the connecting door to check on Lucas. Rudy lay sprawled on the rug. He raised his head, thumped his tail and went back to sleep.

Bathed in the glow of the night-light, Lucas slumbered in the bed that had been his father's. Justin's love-worn, one-eyed teddy bear was clutched under one arm. A knot tightened around Angie's heart. Her little boy was so happy here, as if he'd sensed from the first day that he belonged. This life of privilege was his legacy from the father he'd never known.

Her gaze lingered on Justin's photograph. Justin had been the easy-going twin, happy and fun-loving, charming everyone who knew him. Angie's world had shattered when he died. And now she felt like she'd betrayed him all over again.

Why had she done it? Why had she taken that step? She was powerfully drawn to Jordan, but that was no excuse. There was more at stake here than her own desires. When she'd come to this house, she'd wanted Jordan to respect her as an equal. But she'd blown that out of the water, hadn't she? From here on out, she'd be just another woman who'd tumbled into his bed. How could she face him in the morning?

But there was no avoiding reality. Even if she were to leave she'd still be dealing with Jordan. The best she could do was draw new lines, make new rules and stand behind them.

Blinking away a stray tear, she made a silent vow. Whatever it took, she would be strong. She would prove to herself—and to Jordan—that she could move beyond this night.

Jordan woke at first light. He wasn't surprised to find Angie gone. It made sense that she'd leave to be near Lucas. But how she felt about last night would be anybody's guess. Hell, he wasn't even sure how *he* felt about it.

Swearing under his breath, he flung back the covers. Sprawled naked, he watched dawn creep through the shutters. Angie's crumpled lace panties lay on the sheet beside him, a vivid reminder of the way he'd slid them off her legs and then settled himself between her thighs.

He hadn't meant for last night to happen.

But it had. It had been wonderful and, damn it, he wasn't sorry. If she were here now, he'd like nothing better than to roll her onto her lovely little bum and take up where they'd left off last night.

Unfortunately, the situation wasn't that simple. He'd made Angie a promise when she moved in. That he'd broken it with her full cooperation didn't matter. She had every right to be angry. If she was packing her bags right now, he couldn't blame her.

At best, she'd stay, but things were bound to become awkward between them. Angie was going to need some space. So was he.

Today he had two meetings scheduled in town, but neither was urgent and he was feeling restless. He craved the release of fresh air and hard physical work. Rolling over, he reached for the phone, dialed his office and left a message for the receptionist. The meetings could be rescheduled next week.

With winter around the corner, the hired men would be moving the cattle to the lower pastures, mending the fences and stocking the sheds with hay. The stable needed repairs, as well as a store of oats and fresh straw for the horses. An extra pair of hands wouldn't hurt.

Jordan showered and dressed in jeans and boots. Some time in the saddle would be good for clearing his head. Maybe after that he could make a fresh start with Angie. Meanwhile, some kind of peace offering was in order.

Before he left the house, he had one important phone call to make.

"Was my daddy as nice as Uncle Jordan?"

Angie was on her knees, reaching under the bed for Lucas's lost sneaker. His question slammed her like a fist. She took a moment to grasp the shoe and sit up.

"Your father was every bit as nice but in a different way."

"What way?" Lucas tugged a sock over his foot. His small face was somber.

"Your father loved to make people smile. Everybody liked him."

"Doesn't Uncle Jordan like to make people smile?"

"Your uncle Jordan likes to get things done. He likes being in charge." Angie sighed, knowing her answers wouldn't satisfy a curious little boy.

Lucas frowned as he pulled on his other sock. "You could marry Uncle Jordan. Then he'd be my daddy."

Angie stifled a groan. "I don't think your uncle Jordan would want to marry me."

"Why not?"

Angie thought fast. "Because he likes giving orders. And I don't like taking them."

Lucas mulled over her reply. "Did my daddy like giving you orders?"

"Not so much. Now get your shoes on. Rudy's been in here all night. We need to take him out before breakfast."

They leashed the pup and walked him out to the stable yard. Rudy was proving smart and easy to train. Lucas led his pet to a patch of weedy grass and waited until his business was done. Then Rudy was turned loose to romp in the fenced yard. Jordan had set up his dog's old house under a pine tree. Rudy used it for daily naps but still spent nights in Lucas's room.

There was no sign of Jordan this morning, which was fine, Angie thought. After last night she was in no condition to face him. His touch had driven her wild. She'd responded like an out of control teenager, all common sense blown away in the heat of the moment.

Had Jordan been carried away, too? He'd been so passionate, so intense…yet knowing him as she did, she couldn't help but wonder. Jordan wasn't the type to let desire sweep him away.

Lucas was tossing a stick for Rudy to fetch. Angie

watched them as sunlight crept across the yard. The November morning was crisp and bright, the Sangre de Cristo Mountains dusted with snow. Justin would have wanted his son to grow up in this beautiful place. She owed that much to his memory.

But how was she going to cope with Jordan?

How would she keep from falling into his bed again?

The aromas of bacon and fresh biscuits told her that breakfast was ready. Angie would have been happy to cook for herself and Lucas. But Marta was touchy about her kitchen. Outsiders were not tolerated.

After washing up, they took their places at the kitchen table. Lucas's chatter eased the awkwardness between the two women.

"Did you know my daddy, Miss Marta?"

Marta was wiping the counter. She stiffened at Lucas's question but answered pleasantly enough. "I certainly did. He was a little boy like you when I came here to work."

"What did he look like? Do you have a picture of him?"

"He looked a lot like you. Your uncle Jordan has pictures, but he's out on the range with the cowboys today. Maybe he can show you when he comes home."

Angie wondered if the last words were meant for her. Jordan was clearly making himself scarce. He probably hadn't wanted to face her today—which brought the shoes to mind. This morning she'd opened her bedroom door to find her red stilettos placed neatly on the threshold. Her face had flamed as she remembered leaving them downstairs on the way to Jordan's room. Was it Jordan who'd returned them? Or had it been his eagle-eyed housekeeper?

Either way, she needed to get out of the house for a while. She and Lucas would be attending a party at her cousin's place in town. The break would do her a world of good.

"What did my daddy like to do?" Lucas toyed with his scrambled eggs.

"He liked to play games," Marta said. "And he liked to tease people but in a nice way." Her voice caught. "Everybody loved him."

"Did you know Uncle Jordan, too?"

"Of course I did. They were brothers."

"Did Uncle Jordan like to tease?"

Marta shrugged and went back to her cleaning. "Your uncle Jordan liked to ride his horses."

"Which brother am I like?" Lucas asked.

"You are like your very own self," Angie answered, putting down her fork. "Now, finish your breakfast. I'm taking you into town early to get your hair cut before Ramon's birthday party. You're getting as shaggy as a little sheep dog!"

By the time they were ready to go, it was almost ten. Angie had just enough cash for the haircut, a few gallons of gas and a little gift for her cousin's son, who was having the party. Thank goodness one of her clients would be sending an online payment to her account tomorrow. The last thing she wanted was to depend on Jordan's charity.

With Lucas buckled into his car seat, she started her old blue car. She was backing out of the garage when a lumbering vehicle pulled into the driveway behind her. Slamming on the brake, she turned off the key and opened the door.

The flat-bed tow truck still had its engine running. Bolted onto the bed was a new black SUV, a high-end model she recognized from TV commercials as the ultimate in performance and luxury. The driver was climbing out of the cab. Maybe he was lost.

"Can I help you?" Angie asked, stepping out of the car.

"I'm looking for Miss Angelina Montoya. Would that be you?"

Angie blinked. "Yes, but I don't—"

"Sign here, and I'll unload your vehicle." He thrust a clipboard and a pen toward her. "The title's on the front seat, along with the owner's manual. Key's in the ignition."

"Wait!" Angie pushed the clipboard away. "There's got to be some mistake."

"No mistake. It was bought and paid for this morning by Mr. Jordan Cooper. He said to deliver it to you right away and take your old car. Is he here?"

"No." Angie quivered as her indignation mounted. If Jordan thought he could buy her like some prize heifer...

"There's been a misunderstanding," she told the driver. "Take it back and refund Mr. Cooper's money minus the delivery charge."

Her voice quivered. *Oh, blast, was she going to cry? How could Jordan do this, especially after last night?*

"But Mr. Cooper said to—"

"Take it away!" She stood her ground, glaring up at the startled driver. "I won't accept it! And you're not taking my car!"

Angie's knees sagged as the tow truck roared back down the road. Was Jordan trying to buy her gratitude or reward her for services rendered? Either way, it was a slap in the face.

Turning, she stalked back to her old car. She would drive to town and do her errands as she'd planned. But when Jordan got home, she'd be there waiting. It was time he stopped playing these games with her.

The wind had sharpened, carrying the moist scent of a storm. Jordan turned up the collar of his sheepskin jacket and headed his horse downhill behind the herd. Beef raising was no longer a mainstay of the Cooper Ranch, but the five hundred head of white-faced Herefords provided some income and kept the old traditions alive.

Cutting across the brushy slope, he shooed a few stragglers into line. He would have enjoyed the ranch's early days, when cattle raising was a full-time job and a man could spend days on horseback, camping by the fire and eating off the chuck wagon. Instead, he'd be back in a suit and tie next week, managing the business ventures that kept the ranch in the black.

By now, Angie should have her new SUV—just in time for the trip to town she'd planned to take. He should probably have consulted her first. But things were awkward between them, and with a storm blowing in, he couldn't have her driving the roads in that old blue rattletrap. He could only hope she'd take his gift in the right spirit. All he really wanted was to make sure she and Lucas were safe.

He'd spent most of the morning thinking about last night. Holding Angie in his arms had been pure heaven. The very thought of a repeat engagement was enough to kindle a blaze in his blood. But she wasn't the sort of woman to be kept around as a live-in bed partner. She had too much class for that. And she was too important to him in other ways.

As his thoughts rambled, he'd even weighed the idea of marriage. That would be the simplest way to provide a future for Justin's child—and to keep Angie from running away from him. But there were reasons why it would never work. For one thing, he wasn't great husband material. His brief marriage had proved that. For another, even after last night, he had no reason to believe Angie loved him. Then there was his mother, who would never accept the woman she blamed for Justin's death.

But most compelling of all was the secret truth that lay like a sharp, cold stone inside him. If known, it could destroy his mother and drive Angie away forever.

After getting Lucas's hair cut and shopping for a toy soccer ball, Angie drove to her cousin Raquel's house. Raquel's husband, Antonio Vargas, owned the restaurant where Angie had once worked as a hostess—the restaurant where she'd first met Justin.

The comfortable Vargas home was a few blocks from the restaurant. Ramon, Raquel's five-year-old son, was having a birthday party with pizza, cake and a piñata. Lucas had been invited two weeks ago.

As she watched her son play with his young relatives, Angie reminded herself that this, too, was Lucas's heritage—music and laughter, festive colors and warm *abrazos.* She could no more separate him from this world than from the privileged life that was his father's legacy.

"So will you be staying on the ranch?" Raquel was a few years older than Angie, but the cousins had always been close. She'd gained some weight after four children but was still a pretty woman—and lucky, Angie thought. She and Antonio seemed so happy together.

"It's hard to say," Angie replied. "For now it seems the best thing for Lucas. So many advantages, and he loves it there. But for me…I just don't know." She resisted the urge to fall weeping into her cousin's arms.

"What is it, *querida?*" Raquel's knowing eyes peered into hers. "Is it Jordan? Is it that he looks so much like Justin?"

"No, it's not that at all." And it wasn't, Angie thought. Jordan was a very different man from his brother—and her present state of confusion had nothing to do with his looks. She struggled to put her jumbled feelings into words.

"For years I believed Jordan hated me. Since he discovered Lucas, he's been generous, even kind. But he's also been controlling. It's as if he wants to take over our lives or even take Lucas away from me. I don't know how to deal with him from one day to the next." Angie paused to watch Lucas kick the soccer ball into the miniature net. "This morning he had a brand-new SUV delivered to the ranch for me. I made the driver take it back."

"Why, for heaven's sake? Your old car's a wreck. It isn't even safe to drive."

"How could I accept it, Raquel? It would be as if—" Angie shook her head, unable to continue.

"Is there something you're not telling me?"

"Last night after a party at the house…he'd just broken up with his girlfriend, and one thing led to another. Before I knew it, we were in his bed." She gulped back a surge of emotion. "I made such a fool of myself, Raquel."

"Never mind, what's done is done. And you've lived like a nun for too long." A smile teased Raquel's lips. "Was it good?"

Heat crept into Angie's face. "I'm afraid it was wonderful."

"Are you in love with him?"

"In love? Heavens, no! Jordan Cooper is the most arrogant, manipulative, maddening man I've ever known! And now…" Angie shook her head. "How can I even face him after last night? What can I say to him? If it weren't for Lucas, I'd pack up and leave!"

"Running away won't solve anything, *querida*. All you can do is face up to what happened and be honest. Speak from your heart. That's the only way."

Excusing herself, Raquel hurried off to fetch the cake. Her cousin meant well, Angie told herself. But confronting Jordan and speaking her mind would only make things worse. She'd be better off taking the coward's way out and avoiding the man. Jordan would get the message.

By the time the party ended it was getting dark. Murky clouds roiled out of the west, smelling of snow. Angie shivered as she buckled Lucas into his car seat. Why hadn't she thought to bring warm coats for both of them? But this morning she hadn't been thinking about the weather. Her mind had been on Jordan.

By the time she turned onto the highway out of town, Lucas was fast asleep. Snowflakes as fine as sand peppered the windshield. Angie turned on the wipers. The defroster had died last winter but at least the heater worked. Cranking it up all the way, she pulled into the outside lane and slowed down. With her balding tires, she couldn't risk speeding on the slick asphalt.

Cars flew past her, splattering the windows with sleet.

The drive to the ranch took about forty minutes in good weather. Tonight it would take much longer. She could only hope Lucas would sleep till they got home.

Home... Was that what the Cooper ranch had become?

Angie peered through the flying snow. Maybe she should have accepted the new vehicle. If she had, she and Lucas would be safe. Anything that went wrong now would be her own stubborn fault.

As if thoughts could be prophetic, something in the engine began to clang like an old-fashioned fire alarm. Angie barely had time to pull off the road before the car shuddered into sickening silence.

Angie punched the hazard button, praying the blinking lights would be visible in the storm. Maybe a patrol car would stop to help. If not, she was on her own.

"Mommy, what happened?" Lucas was awake, stirring in his car seat. "What was that noise?"

"That was our car breaking down. Stay where you are while I figure out what to do."

She tried starting the car again. Nothing happened. Reaching for her purse, she fished out her cell phone. The low power indicator was on. She'd be lucky to make one call before the cursed thing died. Why hadn't she charged it last night?

But she knew why, didn't she?

She could dial 911. But this was a broken down car, not a life and death emergency. What if someone failed to get desperately needed help because the police were answering her call?

She could phone Raquel. But Antonio would be at work. Raquel would have to leave her children to drive this dangerous road in the storm—something Angie would never ask her to do.

She could wait for help to happen by. But the night was cold. Soon the car's battery would run out. With no lights, how would other drivers even know they were there, much less that they needed help?

That left her with just one option. Cringing at the thought, she found Jordan's card in her purse and punched in his cell phone number. She held her breath as the phone rang once, then again.

Please, she prayed silently. He had to pick up. He just *had* to.

Seven

Jordan had come in from the range at dusk and put away his horse. By then the snow was flying. He was tired and chilled but at least he wouldn't have to drive on slick roads tonight. He was ready for a good meal, a hot shower and an early bedtime.

The thought of driving turned his mind to Angie again and to the gift he'd purchased. Would Angie be grateful for the new SUV? Or had he overstepped? Lord knows, with winter coming she'd need something safe. But Angie was capable of taking his gift in the wrong spirit. However she might have taken it, he was about to find out.

As he neared the back door, Rudy came bounding across the yard. What was the pup doing here? It wasn't like Lucas to leave his beloved pet out in the cold. Letting the dog into the enclosed back porch, Jordan poured some kibble into a bowl before he entered the house.

Marta was in the kitchen. One look at her worried face told him something was wrong.

"Where's Angie?" he asked.

"She took Lucas into town this morning, but it's getting late. They should've been back by now."

"Did the dealer deliver her new vehicle?"

"Yes. But she made the man take it back. She left in her old car."

Jordan swore under his breath. He should've known Angie would be too proud to accept his gift. If anything had happened to them in this storm…

The jangle of his cell phone broke into his thoughts.

"Jordan?" Angie's voice was so faint through the static that he could barely hear what she was saying. Something about breaking down on the road.

"Hang on, I'm on my way," he said. "Where are you?"

He waited for her reply. Only silence remained on the line. Calling her back didn't work, either. Damned phone was probably in the same condition as her car. Miss Angelina Montoya was going to get an earful when he found her.

If he found her before anything else went wrong.

Jordan lowered his high-beam headlights to reduce the glare against the falling snow. He was driving the ranch's heavy-duty club cab pickup. In the backseat was a box filled with warm blankets and snacks, which Marta had pressed on him at the last minute.

As he drove, black scenarios flashed through his mind—Angie's car off the road, maybe stuck in a ditch or even wrecked. Angie and Lucas cold and scared, maybe hurt, with no help—or worse, at the mercy of any criminals who happened by.

She hadn't told him where she was. But he had to assume she'd been headed home, which meant she'd be on the opposite side of the four-lane road. If he didn't slow down, he could miss seeing her. Would her lights be on? The shoulder of the road was narrow, with a steep drop-off. With no lights, someone could easily hit her, knocking the car down the slope, maybe rolling it…

Damn!

Reaching for his cell, he dialed the highway patrol. The dispatcher had no report of a blue sedan off the road. She promised to put out an alert, but the first big snow of the season was always bad for accidents. The officers would be busy tonight.

He'd gone halfway to town and was wondering if he'd missed her when he spotted the low shape off the far side of the pavement. Dark windows caught the reflected gleam of passing headlights. Jordan broke into a cold sweat as he found a wide spot, swung the truck around and pulled up behind the old blue sedan. Would they be there? Would they be all right?

Leaving his headlights on, he climbed out of the truck. Dread clutched his throat as he walked toward the car. There was no movement inside, no sign of life.

Only when he brushed the snow off the driver's window and peered inside did he see them. They were huddled on the floor in front of the passenger seat—both of them alive and safe. *Thank God.*

Angie watched from the warm truck as Jordan released the brake on her old car and pushed it down the embankment where no one would hit it in the dark.

He'd barely spoken to her as he bundled Lucas in a blanket, mounted his car seat in the back and buckled him in. But the words would come—she had no doubt of that. And she would take her punishment like bitter medicine. Everything that had gone wrong tonight had been her fault.

She glanced back at Lucas. He'd eaten a cookie and was already falling asleep. But earlier, in the car, he'd been so cold and scared. It was her job to keep her son safe. How could she have put him through this?

Jordan lingered on the edge of the road, gazing down at the car. Silhouetted in the headlights and surrounded with swirling snow, he made a solitary figure. That was how she'd always seen him, Angie recalled. Justin had been the sociable twin, surrounded by friends. But aside from the women who moved in and out of his life, Jordan had been a loner.

Angie had assumed he wanted things that way. Now, for the first time, she was struck by his isolation.

Slowly he turned and walked back toward the truck. In the headlights, his face was etched with weary shadows. Angie braced herself for the tirade that was sure to come once they were on the road. She waited as he climbed into the driver's seat and closed the door. She waited as he shifted and pulled back onto the asphalt. He drove in silence, his mouth a grim line.

"I'm sorry, Jordan," Angie said at last.

"You should be." He kept his eyes on the road. "Taking a chance on that old car—you're damned lucky nothing worse happened. Why didn't you keep the vehicle I had delivered?"

A tear stole down Angie's cheek. "You know why I didn't keep it."

"I wanted you and Lucas to be safe. And I believe in buying the best. What's wrong with that?"

Her resolve to take her scolding quietly vanished as her temper rose. "What's wrong is that you didn't ask me! I don't make a practice of accepting $50,000 gifts—

especially from a man I just…" She choked on the final words.

"Is that why you sent it back? Because you'd slept with me? Did you think it was some sort of payment? Good Lord, Angie—"

"What was I supposed to think? I'm trying to make this arrangement work for Lucas's sake, but I won't be bought, Jordan. I won't be your mistress!"

"I can't believe this." He slowed down as if to pull off the road, then seemed to change his mind. "I'd never try to buy you, Angie, or any other woman. Your safety and Lucas's—that was my only motive."

Angie studied his stern profile, her mind working. "If that's true, I have a suggestion. Hear me out."

"I'm listening." His eyes narrowed but he kept his gaze straight ahead.

"One thing we both agree on—I need a safe vehicle for Lucas. In the next few days, you can take me to a dealer you trust. I'll pick out a solid, reliable *used* car with four-wheel drive, one that costs, maybe, one-fourth as much as that behemoth you picked out for me."

"Angie, I can afford to pay for a new car."

"But *I* can't, and I want it to be *my* car. If you don't mind loaning me the cash, I'll buy it myself and work off the debt. There must be something I can do around the place—sweep the stable, oil the tack—"

"Don't be silly." She was relieved to note, though, that her attempt at humor had worked. He looked less forbidding than he had before. He was silent for a moment. "How are you at filing and bookkeeping?"

"Fair enough. I keep records for my own business."

"Then you've got a job if you want it. The accounts for the ranch need more attention than I have time to give them. I could honestly use your help."

"You're not just making up work for me?"

"Hardly. I'll be glad to hand it off to you. We can figure out your hours and wages tomorrow, after we've had a good night's sleep."

The very mention of the word *sleep* made her pulse lurch. Did he think she was going to spend another night in his bed?

"Let's clear the air about something." He spoke as if he'd read her mind. "I enjoyed last night, and I hope you did, too. But it was just a good time, with no strings attached. You're welcome back any time. But only on those same terms and only if it's what you want. As for that Victorian blather about becoming my mistress…"

He let the words hang in the silence. Angie felt the flames creep higher in her face. Jordan deserved a sound slap for what he'd just said. But he was driving on a winter slicked road, with Lucas asleep in the back. She willed her voice to sound cold and flat.

"As far as I'm concerned, last night never happened. And as long as we're clearing the air, there's one thing you need to understand. Lucas is my son, not yours. If this so-called arrangement doesn't work out and I end up leaving, he goes with me. I won't let you have him."

She heard the sharp intake of his breath. She'd wanted to wound him, and she had. So why did she find herself wishing she hadn't opened her mouth?

A beat of silence passed between them before he spoke. "We both have Lucas's best interests at heart. For now, we'll just have to trust each other to make the right choices."

"Fine." *Whatever that meant.* Jordan had given her an answer that could be read in any number of ways. Was he scheming to edge her out of the picture and keep Lucas to raise as his heir? A month ago, she'd have believed that easily…but now she just wasn't sure. Either way, if he thought she'd give up her son for any reason, the man had a great deal to learn about a mother's love.

What had Jordan's own mother been like growing up? Angie remembered Meredith Cooper as a woman who carried herself like a queen, exquisitely dressed and coiffed, with her historic house, her prestigious marriage and her perfect sons.

She had treated Angie with a coldness that bordered on contempt. How much of that coldness had come from a perceived need to protect her beloved Justin? Now that Angie had a child of her own, she felt a measure of understanding. But she knew better than to think that a shift in her own attitude would make any difference to the woman who had been so determined to hate her even before Justin's death. Sooner or later, Meredith Cooper would learn that the woman who'd brought Justin down was living in her house. However it came about, things were bound to get ugly.

Could she depend on Jordan to stand up to his formidable mother? She gazed at his chiseled profile, silhouetted against the snowy glass. Jordan knew how to get what he wanted, and he had his share of Meredith's steel. But would it be enough?

She'd be wise to prepare herself for the worst.

Ahead, through the snow-speckled darkness, Angie could see the lights of the house. Weariness swept over her as Jordan pulled into the garage and switched off the engine. Right now, all she wanted was to put Lucas to bed and go to sleep.

Jordan unbuckled Lucas from his car seat and lifted him gently in his arms. Lucas's eyes blinked open. "Where's Rudy?" he muttered.

"Rudy's on the back porch. I'll bring him up after

you're in bed." Jordan carried the drowsy little boy across the patio and up the stairs to his room. Angie followed, stopping him at the door.

"I can handle things from here," she said.

"All right. I'll go get the dog." He passed Lucas to her waiting arms, then turned and walked away without another word. Angie took her son to the bathroom and maneuvered him into his pajamas. She was so tired she could barely think, but it filtered through her mind that she hadn't thanked Jordan for coming to their rescue and possibly saving their lives. She would remedy that when he came back—*if* he came back. He'd probably had enough of her for the night.

She'd just finished tucking Lucas into bed when she heard the doorknob turn. The door opened just far enough to admit Rudy, who trotted over to the rug and curled up in his usual spot.

Angie heard the door click shut and the fading sound of Jordan's boot heels on the tiles. Impulsively she opened the door and darted out into the dark hallway.

"Jordan!" The name was whispered, not shouted, but he turned around. In silhouette, his shoulders sagged with weariness.

Closing the door behind her, Angie walked toward him.

What now? Was she coming to take another piece out of his hide? Jordan braced himself for a storm. "Make it fast," he growled. "I'm dead on my feet."

She halted a step away. Melted snowflakes glimmered in her dark hair. Heaven help him, even after a night of driving him crazy, she was beautiful. "This won't take long," she said. "I just wanted to thank you. Anything could've happened to us out there on the road. But you answered and came when I called." A smile teased her ripe lips. "That makes you a hero in my book."

Jordan fought the urge to crush her in his arms and kiss her till she begged for mercy. Did the woman have any idea how she'd scared him or what a relief it had been to find her and Lucas safe? Only tonight had he realized how important the two of them had become—more important than he'd ever let on.

He willed himself not to touch her—if he did, he'd be lost. "Get some sleep," he said. "In the morning we'll put this night behind us and start fresh. All right?"

"All right." She seemed hesitant. But he had to leave now, while he could.

"Good night, Angie." He turned and walked away. As he reached the top of the stairs he heard her door close. He forced himself to keep walking and to focus on the tasks at hand instead of memories of her lush body in his arms. Tomorrow he would set up the books for her in his home office. Then he'd take her to town to buy a car. *Her* car—one she could afford to keep if she left him.

Every day with Angie seemed to be a new battleground. But he had to do right by her and Lucas—and by his mother, too. He could never make up for the terrible loss they'd suffered. But trying could be his only hope of redemption.

In her room, Angie stripped off her sweater and jeans. She was weary to the bone but her pulse was still racing.

Had it been a mistake, calling Jordan back to thank him? They'd snarled at each other most of the way home. And he'd been none too friendly when she'd faced him in the hallway. But even as he scowled at her, something had been there—and she'd responded like a hormone-crazed teenager. It was as if every part of her body remembered last night in his bed and was craving more of the same.

You're welcome back anytime. But only on those same terms and only if it's what you want.

His words came back to mock her. Was that what she wanted, another wild night of recreational sex with no strings attached? Or, heaven help her, did she want it to mean something?

Are you in love with him?

Now it was Raquel's voice she heard in her head. But the question was useless. Angie knew what love was. She'd loved Justin with all her heart and soul. What she felt with Jordan was more like…what? Lust? Need? A burning ring of fire?

You're welcome back anytime.

She stood trembling on the rug, heat shimmering through her veins. It would be so easy—and the release would feel so good.

One hand reached for the doorknob, paused then dropped to her side. She knew better, Angie chided herself. Another visit to Jordan's bed would only weaken her in his eyes—and cheapen her in her own. Aside from a fleeting pleasure, nothing good could come of it.

With a sigh, she reached for her nightgown, pulled it on and slipped into bed. There were things she wanted from life—a home to call her own, brothers and sisters for Lucas and a good man to love her.

That man would not be Jordan Cooper.

Eight

Jordan began bracing himself as he pulled into the parking lot of the retirement community where his mother lived. Their confrontation was bound to be emotional. But he couldn't put it off any longer—not unless he wanted to lie.

The *Peralta,* as the place was known, was the most exclusive senior residence in Santa Fe. Located off Canyon Road, within strolling distance of art galleries and restaurants, the gated complex was a maze of pueblo-style architecture, patios and gardens. The wealthiest residents lived in luxury, with staff on hand for their every need.

Last week's snow had already melted. Jordan's path took him past the spa, the tennis courts and the club house. There were plenty of activities to be found here, but despite his urging his mother showed no interest in them. Jordan worried that she was sinking into depression. But she refused to socialize or to be seen by a doctor. Meredith Cooper had made up her mind to be miserable.

Taking the elevator to the second floor of the building, he rang her doorbell. She buzzed him in with the remote control she kept by her chair.

"Hello, Jordan." As usual, she was impeccably coiffed and dressed, her nails freshly manicured, her upswept hair sculpted into platinum waves and her silk blouse tucked neatly into pleated designer slacks. Her balcony overlooked a small lake lined with cattails, where migrating ducks and geese sheltered on their journey south. But drawn curtains blocked the view. Too much sun was the excuse she gave.

He walked across the room and took her hand. She'd always been formal with her sons. "How have you been this week, Mother?"

"So-so." She shrugged her thin shoulders.

"I thought we could go to lunch at *La Fonda* today," he said. "The sun's out, and I've reserved a table. Come on, I'll get your coat."

She cast him a withering look. "Have you forgotten that today's the anniversary of your father's death? How could you even think of going out to eat?"

Actually he *had* forgotten. His only thought had been to get her out of this gloomy suite, to someplace where it might be easier to talk. "I can drive you to the cemetery," he said. "We could buy flowers on the way."

"I don't feel up to going out. And the cemetery would only make me feel worse." She sighed, clasping her arthritic hands in her lap. "How are things at the ranch these days?"

It was the opening Jordan needed. Pulling up a chair he sat down. "I've got some surprising news," he said. "It seems you have a grandson."

Her eyes narrowed. "You—?"

"No. He's not mine. The boy is Justin's. Angie was pregnant when he died."

Her face had gone ashen. For the space of a breath she looked vulnerable. Then her features hardened. "How convenient," she said. "My son dies, and four years later that hussy shows up with a child who could be anybody's. I suppose she's asking for money."

Jordan squelched an angry retort. His mother had endured terrible losses—first her favorite son, then her husband who'd suffered a stroke the week of Justin's death and lingered, bedridden, for nine months before passing away. He could hardly blame her for being bitter. He willed himself to be patient.

"Angie's not asking for a thing," he said. "And she didn't show up. I tracked her down." He summarized the story of how he'd found Angie on the internet.

"Did you think to check the birth record?"

"I have a copy in the car. The date fits, and Justin is listed as the father."

"And you've had DNA testing done?"

"No need. Aside from his mother's coloring, the boy's all Cooper. You'll agree when you meet him."

She pressed her hand to her forehead, as if fending off a headache. "Why should I want to meet him? Haven't I suffered enough pain already without some illegitimate brat reminding me of my son? Write the woman a check and be done with it."

Jordan controlled the impulse to leap to his feet and shout at her. He loved his mother, but how could anyone be so callous?

"Lucas is your grandson—an innocent little boy who's not to blame for any of this mess. If you turn your back on him, Mother, you'll regret it for the rest of your life."

Her mouth quirked in a bitter smile. "I can see the child's already won you over. What about the mother? I recall that she was pretty. Has she bewitched you the way she did your brother?"

Jordan had anticipated the question. Even so, his reaction was physical—a flash of heat like a slap to the face. "I'm trying to do right by Justin's son," he said. "As the boy's mother, Angie's part of the package."

"Meaning...?" His mother's eyes were as sharp as a hawk's.

"They're living at the ranch—at my invitation."

Her reaction was exactly what he'd expected. It was as if he'd dropped a live grenade in her lap. But he had to give her credit for a swift recovery.

"That's unacceptable!" she snapped.

"Is it? If Justin had lived long enough to get married, they'd be his wife and son. Whether you like it or not, they're family."

"Not to me. I want nothing to do with them."

Jordan shook his head. "Look at it this way, Mother. Without them, our family consists of two people—you and me. If I don't remarry and start siring the next generation of little Coopers—and I don't foresee that happening—we're dinosaurs. The Cooper line and Cooper legacy will end for good."

"This isn't funny, Jordan. I'd like you to leave now."

"Fine." Jordan rose. "Think about what I've told you. I'll give you a call later in the week."

He'd reached the door when she called his name. He turned back to face her.

"Thanksgiving's two weeks away," she said. "You'll be here to have dinner with me as usual, won't you?"

Jordan had seen this coming, too. "No," he said. "We're having Thanksgiving at the ranch. You're more than welcome to come. I'll even send a car for you. But if you choose to stay here, you'll be eating without me."

She stared at him, shocked into silence for once.

"Think about it. You can let me know next week." With that, Jordan was out the door, closing it behind him.

His mother wasn't a bad person, he reminded himself. She could be generous, even loving when she chose to. But she was protective of her personal wounds, refusing to let them heal. Lucas could be her salvation—but only if she'd let the little boy into her heart.

Jordan was doing his best to make that happen. Today he'd taken the first step. But he was facing an uphill battle. His mother might accept Lucas, who was, after all, her own flesh and blood. But Angie?

Lord, what had he gotten himself into?

He arrived home to find Angie updating the books in his office. After only a week, Jordan was beginning to wonder how he'd managed without her. His messy male sanctuary had taken on an air of calm efficiency, with everything in perfect order. Something about her presence lent warmth to the cold space. When she wasn't there, he missed it.

She seemed to be settling in. With his help she'd bought a sturdy four-year-old sport wagon, which she used to come and go as she pleased. She'd also enrolled Lucas in preschool to give him new friends and free up her time. Jordan was learning that the best way to keep Angie happy was to give her plenty of space. For now their fragile truce appeared to be working.

But it was about to be tested.

She glanced up as he stepped into the open doorway, a hint of a smile on her face. Dressed in a lacy pink cardigan over a black shirt, she looked soft and delectable.

Since the night of the party, Jordan had managed to keep his hands off the woman. But his thoughts were harder to control. He deserved a black eye for what was going through his mind right now.

She'd tucked a lock of her hair behind one ear, revealing a tiny pearl stud. He pictured himself bending across the desk, catching her silky earlobe in his mouth and nibbling till she moaned, then grazing his way down her throat to the open collar of her blouse and—

"Do you need your desk, Jordan?" she asked. "I can always come back and finish this later."

Jordan jerked himself back to full attention. His wandering imagination was driving him crazy. If he didn't get a rein on his thoughts, he'd be in serious trouble.

The hard reality was, he wanted this woman. He wanted her back in his arms and back in his bed. But first she'd have to want him. That was going to take some time.

Meanwhile there were other issues to be faced.

Jordan wasn't exactly helping her concentration. Angie tried to focus on the computer, where she was entering receipts and invoices into a programmed table. Because she was getting paid by the hour, and because he hadn't asked her to leave the office, she could only assume she should go on working. But he wasn't making it easy.

She could feel his gaze on her. Was he undressing her with those mesmerizing gray eyes, remembering how she'd looked without her clothes? Was he remembering what his hands had touched, what his lips had tasted and how it had felt when his swollen sex had pushed inside her?

She was. And she had to stop.

Angie forced herself to meet his eyes. "Is there something I can do for you, Jordan?" she asked.

His mouth twitched slightly, and she realized what she'd said. *Blast the man!* She tried again.

"I really want to finish these entries before the van lets Lucas off, so unless you—"

"The entries can wait." He walked into the room, pulled a chair up to the desk and sat down. "I need a word with you," he said.

Her pulse skittered. Then she saw the serious expression on his face. "Is something wrong?"

"Nothing I hadn't planned on. I paid a visit to my mother today."

A leaden sensation stirred in Angie's stomach. She was just beginning to feel at home here, and Lucas was blossoming. But one word from Meredith Cooper could change it all. "So she knows about Lucas—and about me."

"She was still in shock when I left. It's going to take some time for her to come around."

"*If* she comes around. I can just imagine how she feels about my living in her house."

"This isn't about how she feels. It's about doing the right thing for Justin's son."

"Is that what you told her?"

"In so many words. And I made it clear that you were part of the package."

"I see." Angie gazed past him to the photo of the two brothers with their string of fish. Jordan had offered to take it down, but she'd told him to leave it. Lucas often wandered into the office, and he loved seeing that picture.

"I invited Mother here for Thanksgiving," Jordan said. "I won't have her answer until next week, but I think it's time she met her grandson."

"*No!*" Angie reacted like a lioness with a threatened cub. "If your mother dislikes me, I can accept that. But I won't have her venting her spite on Lucas!"

Jordan's gaze was calm. "My mother prides herself on her good manners. Whatever she might be thinking, she won't do anything to make a scene."

"You can't guarantee that. My cousin Raquel's invited us to her house. We'll go there, so you and your mother can have this place to yourselves."

Jordan's eyes were storm clouds, troubled and unsettling. "Be still and listen, Angie. There are things you need to understand—things I should probably have told you sooner."

"Like why you brought us here in the first place?"

"That's part of it." He exhaled, shifting on his chair. "This property and most of the other family assets are in a trust. When my father suffered his stroke, the trusteeship passed to my mother. Justin and I were listed as heirs."

"So all this is about money?"

"Hear me out. I owe it to my brother to do the right thing—the thing he'd want done if he'd lived. Justin's name is still listed on the trust document. If I can get Lucas declared his legal heir, Justin's share of the trust will go to him."

Angie stared at him. "But as things stand, wouldn't everything go to you, Jordan? Why would you want to change that?"

"Because I owe that much to Justin's memory." He shrugged. "Besides, I've made plenty of money on my own. It's not as if I need to be greedy."

"And your mother?" Angie felt as if her face had gone numb. She forced her lips to shape the question.

"Mother could make things difficult if she chose to. I could probably win in court, but I don't want to fight her, and I don't want to wait years for her to pass away. My best hope is that she'll accept Lucas as her grandson and add him to the trust herself."

"So that's why you invited her here."

"In part, yes."

"And you're hoping Lucas will win her over. That's an awful burden to place on a little boy."

His gaze and voice softened. "I know, Angie. But it's not just about the money. I want her to know Lucas for his own sake—and for hers. My mother's a good woman, but she has a broken heart. Having a grandson to love could make all the difference for her."

Angie stared down at her hands on the desk. "She could hurt him, Jordan. Hurt my sweet little boy. How can I risk that?"

"My mother is protective, not cruel. Think of the good that could come of this—for both of them."

"I just don't know...." She looked up to meet his probing gaze. "How can I be a party to this? Your mother always believed I was after Justin's money. She'll think this whole thing was my idea—and she'll fight it."

His hand slid across the desk to rest on hers, the palm cool and lightly callused. The contact sent a quiver of awareness up her arm.

"It's only Thanksgiving dinner," he said. "There'll be time for the rest later on, but we have to start somewhere."

Could he feel her galloping pulse? Angie shook her head. "Your mother blames me for Justin's death and your father's stroke. How can I even face her?"

His fingers tightened around hers, their grip almost painful. "If she still blames you, it's time she stopped. And it's time you stopped blaming yourself. You didn't crash that plane, Angie. And you didn't do anything to my father. Nobody knows that better than I do."

Angie stared at him, her throat jerking tight. Jordan had been the last one in the family to see his brother alive. Did he know something she didn't?

Nobody knows that better than I do.

She could confront him, demand to be told what, if anything, he was hiding. But if the secret was so terrible that he'd kept it all these years, did she really want to know?

The sound of a horn in the driveway broke into her thoughts. The van from Bright Tots Preschool was waiting for someone to come out and meet Lucas. With a murmured apology to Jordan, she rose and rushed out of the room. Her son would be bubbling over with enthusiasm as he showed her his artwork and activity sheets and told her about his new friends. She wanted to give him her full attention.

Jordan's plan would have to wait.

Jordan stood at the window, watching as Angie raced down the drive. The wind bannered her long black hair as she ran, feet light, arms open to greet her son. She was like a stained-glass window, transparent and glowing, both inside and out. He saw no deceit in her, no greed, no selfishness, only love for her child—his brother's child.

Angie deserved to hear the truth about Justin's death. A moment ago he'd come within a breath of telling her. But then he'd thought the better of it. Telling her now could shatter his plans.

He had little doubt his mother would come to the ranch for Thanksgiving. Despite her protests, she'd be too curious to stay away. It would be up to him to see that things went smoothly.

He had two weeks to build bridges of trust—bridges that could ease the way to healing what was left of his family. He owed it to all the lives his hasty words had destroyed—to Justin and his father, to his mother, to Lucas…and to Angie.

He had to make this work.

* * *

"Can I see the pictures of my daddy tonight, Uncle Jordan?"

At her son's question, Angie glanced at Jordan across the dinner table. Lucas had been asking to see the Cooper family album since the morning Marta mentioned the photos. So far, Jordan had been busy. Tonight he gave the boy a smile.

"I've got time—that is, if your mother says it's all right."

"Am I included?" Angie asked.

"I wouldn't have it any other way."

"Fine, then. But finish your dinner first, Lucas." It might be painful for her, looking at pictures of Justin and Justin's family, she thought. But Lucas was bound to have questions later. It would be helpful to know what he'd seen.

After dinner, Jordan lit the fireplace, and the three of them settled on the sofa—Lucas in the middle with the leather-bound photo album on his lap. Someone had arranged each page of photos with corner mounts, documenting them with little handwritten notes. Meredith? Who else could it have been? Like everything else in the house, the album had her exquisite touch.

On the first page was a portrait of a handsome bridal couple. "Those are your grandparents, Lucas," Jordan said.

"Are they dead?" Lucas understood that Angie's parents had died in a wreck when she was in her teens.

"Your grandfather is. But your grandmother is very much alive. Maybe you'll get to meet her soon. Of course, she's older now."

Angie studied the photo over Lucas's shoulder. Braxton Cooper as a younger man had looked much like his sons. Meredith had been a beauty with rich auburn hair, a model's figure and a face worthy of a magazine cover. How happy they looked. Strange, Angie had never thought of Justin's staid, snobbish parents as having been in love.

"Who are those babies?" Lucas had turned the page. The infant boys lying on a sheepskin rug were identical. Either of them could've been Lucas at that age.

Jordan's laugh sounded forced. "The grumpy one's me. And the one who's smiling is your father."

"How can you tell?"

"I just can."

More pages, more photographs—two little boys in the arms of their beautiful mother. Two little boys in the bath. Two little boys playing with their puppy. At three the twins had been fair-haired. Aside from that, they were the very image of Lucas—the unruly cowlick, the dimpled left cheek, the stubborn chin.

Later pictures gave Angie glimpses of how her son would look as he grew older. She glanced at Jordan. This had to be painful for him, too, reliving the years with his lost brother. She'd always heard that twins had a connection so strong that no separation, even death, could break it. That might explain why he was so determined to carry out what he believed to be Justin's wishes.

The news that he planned to make Lucas his brother's heir had surprised and touched her. Still, she couldn't help questioning his motives. Was he acting out of generosity? Guilt? Some other motive?

Only one thing was certain. Jordan Cooper never did anything without a good reason.

"Who's that?" Lucas had turned to the last page in the album. Angie found herself staring down at Jordan's wedding portrait. The bride was a beauty with sun-streaked hair, cornflower eyes and a willowy figure. Her simple gown was exquisitely cut, most likely a designer original. The diamond ring on her left hand would have dazzled a Hollywood starlet.

"That's my wife," Jordan muttered in answer to Lucas's question. "Or was. I've never gotten around to taking that picture out of the album."

"Did she die like my daddy?"

"No. She just went away."

"She's beautiful," Angie said.

"Yes. Just ask her second husband."

Angie stole another glance at the wedding photo. Jordan's mouth was smiling but not his eyes. He looked as if he'd already known how the marriage would end.

Had he loved his bride? Was he even capable of loving a woman for a lifetime?

Once he'd implied that he'd married out of duty, to continue the family line. It hadn't worked out. So now he was trying something else—bringing in a ready-made heir. She believed that he genuinely cared about Lucas. But if he thought he was acting in the boy's best interests, he might still use Lucas as a tool in his quest to carry out his family obligation.

What would she do if she found proof they were being used?

Would she have the courage to leave?

Nine

Raquel answered Angie's call on the second ring. "What is it, *querida?*" she demanded. "Is something wrong?"

"No, everything's fine. At least I hope so." Angie leaned back in her chair, flexing her tired shoulders. She'd spent the past two hours working on a new website for a client and she was ready for a break.

"You don't sound like everything's fine. Is Jordan treating you all right?"

Angie sighed, wondering how much she dared tell her inquisitive cousin. "Jordan's been on good behavior lately. Strictly hands off."

"That's too bad. No wonder you don't sound very happy."

Angie willed herself to ignore her cousin's teasing—and the rush of heat to her face. "That's not why I'm calling. I'm afraid Lucas and I won't be coming to your house for Thanksgiving tomorrow."

There was a pause on the line. "Please tell me that man is taking you to Hawaii!"

"Don't I wish!" Angie had to chuckle. "No, Jordan invited his mother to come to the ranch and meet Lucas. We just got word that she'll be here for Thanksgiving dinner."

"What? The Dragon Lady herself?"

"You're incorrigible, Raquel! Don't ever let Lucas hear you call her that."

"I'll try to hold my tongue around him. But after the way the woman treated you—"

"I can't dwell on the past," Angie said. "She's Lucas's grandmother. I've got to give her a chance."

"But will she give *you* a chance? Take my advice, *chica*. Hide the sharp knives, and don't turn your back on her."

"Advice taken." Angie nudged the subject in a different direction. "You should see this place. It's like the return of the Queen to Buckingham Palace. Everything washed and dusted and polished. Marta even took me up on my offer to clean the upstairs and sweep the leaves off of the patio."

"Speaking of Marta, is she still treating you like you've broken in to steal the silverware?"

"Oh, she can be prickly. But at least I know where she stands. She adored Justin, and part of her still blames me..." Angie's voice faltered for an instant. "She seems to care about Lucas. That's all that matters."

"Is it? Are you really happy there?"

"Lucas is happy. That's enough for now."

Ending the call with a promise to visit soon, Angie put down the phone, rose to stretch her legs and walked to the window. From her upstairs room she could see past the top of the garage to where Jordan was just pulling the pickup into the drive. He'd taken Lucas out on the range with him to deliver some salt and hay to the cattle. Angie's son had been over the moon at the prospect of doing real cowboy work.

Jordan climbed out of the truck and helped the little boy out of his car seat in the back. Lucas was dressed in a plaid shirt and denim jacket, blue jeans and the cowboy boots and hat Jordan had bought him. As they came up the walk to the front door, Angie noticed how he matched Jordan's stride and mimicked his style of walking.

Her son had found the father figure he'd missed so much. But Jordan wasn't Lucas's father. He was a man with his own agenda. Even if he didn't mean to harm Lucas, it could still happen all too easily. Jordan had spent little time around children. Did he have any idea how vulnerable a child could be? His generous plan to include Lucas in the family trust could ensure the boy's future. But what about Lucas's trusting young heart?

Hurrying her steps, she reached the top of the staircase as they came in through the front door. Lucas was flushed with cold and excitement. He was grinning, chattering away as he gazed up at his hero.

Angie was halfway down the stairs before her son noticed her. Breaking away from Jordan, he raced up the steps. "Mama, I helped Uncle Jordan feed the cows! A calf sucked on my finger! It tickled!"

"My goodness!" She sat down on the step, aware of Jordan watching as she boosted Lucas onto her lap.

"I think your boy's got the makings of a rancher," he said. "He's already a good hand with the cattle."

"That doesn't surprise me one bit." Angie's gaze took in Jordan's wind-burned face, thick flannel shirt and long denim-clad legs. He looked like a man in his element, fit and strong and ready for action. A little whorl of desire uncurled in the depths of her body.

How could she protect her son from Jordan's spell—when she couldn't even protect herself?

He could get used to this, Jordan thought. The warm house, the smell of hot soup and fresh-baked pies wafting from the kitchen, Angie with her happy little boy looking down at him from the staircase. The moment was like a glimpse of heaven—but only a glimpse. Glance away and it would vanish like a mirage.

He'd be a fool to think his life could be anything but what it was—a balancing act between family obligations, his business and the ranch. Get Lucas added to the trust, with a regular income, and his duty to his brother would be done. Angie could stay here as long as she liked. But she wouldn't stay forever. Beyond Lucas's welfare, she had no life here and no future. Sooner or later, she would choose to move on.

Still, looking up at her, he felt a raw hunger for what he couldn't have—not just for her body, but for all the intimate things she'd never shared with him. He wanted her to trust him, to confide in him, to depend on him…. But that would demand the same openness on his part. It wasn't going to happen.

Tomorrow his mother would be coming to dinner. Once again he'd be doing the balancing act, keeping things calm, steering the talk in safe directions. So much depended on making sure the afternoon ended with everyone smiling and civil.

He could hardly wait for the blasted day to be over.

Thanksgiving Day had dawned with chalky clouds and spatters of snow. The weather matched Angie's mood. Given the choice between sharing a meal with Meredith

Cooper and trudging barefoot through a winter blizzard, she'd have gladly chosen the latter.

At least Marta had welcomed her help today. Not only were they cooking dinner for the household, but also for the hired men who hadn't gone home and would be dining in the kitchen. There was a twenty-five-pound stuffed turkey, a half dozen pies, several pans of Marta's wonderful rolls, a small mountain of potatoes and much more.

Angie felt her anxiety rising as she surveyed the end of the long dining room table. The four elegant place settings looked lonely, she thought. It was too bad the hired help couldn't be invited to eat in here, filling some of the empty chairs. But Meredith would never stand for such a thing.

Lucas came down the stairs, scrubbed, combed and dressed in clothes that Angie hoped would stay clean through dinner. "It smells yummy!" he said. "When do we get to eat?"

"Not until Uncle Jordan gets here with your grandmother. Did you remember to feed Rudy?"

"Uh-huh."

"And do you remember what you learned about manners?"

"Say please and thank you," the boy recited. "Don't talk with your mouth full. Don't eat with your fingers—is it ok to eat bread with your fingers, Mama?"

"As long as you don't play with it. Go on."

"Wipe your hands and face on your napkin, not your shirt." He frowned, his dark brows knitting like Jordan's. "Is that all?"

"Just one more thing. When grownups are talking, you should be quiet and let them finish. Don't interrupt. All right?"

"All…right." He swung away, distracted by a sound

from the front of the house. "They're here, Mama! They're here!"

Angie forced herself to remain in the dining room, watching as he bounded into the entry. He stood frozen as the front door swung open and Meredith Cooper stepped over the threshold.

She was as regal as ever—tall in chic high-heeled boots and a sweeping camel's hair coat. But she was thinner and older than Angie remembered, her skin turning to crepe, her sharp eyes sunk into hollows. The hands that clasped her designer bag were swollen at the knuckles.

Jordan came in behind her, closed the door and stepped forward to lift Lucas in his arms, bringing the boy to eye level with his imperious grandmother. Angie held her breath in silent prayer. It was like watching her child face down a lioness.

"Mother," Jordan said, "this is Lucas, your grandson."

Lucas put out his right hand. "How do you do," he said in a small mechanical voice.

Angie swallowed a gasp. The formal response was so unlike her son. Evidently she hadn't been the only one coaching him.

Meredith's lips tightened in a wintry smile. Taking Lucas's small hand in her arthritic fingers, she gave it a brief shake. "I'm pleased to meet you, Lucas," she said.

"I believe dinner's almost ready." Jordan lowered Lucas to the floor. "Will you let us take your coat and bag?" Without waiting for a reply, he eased the coat off her shoulders and handed the purse to Lucas. Together they set off down the hall toward the back bedrooms.

Leaving Angie to face the lioness alone.

Meredith walked into the dining room. "Hello, Angelina," she said. "I can't say I ever expected to see you here again."

Angie stood her ground. "I never expected to be here. But when Jordan found us, he insisted that Lucas get to know his father's family."

"I see." Meredith fussed with the settings, refolding the linen napkins, frowning down at the Winnie the Pooh cup in Lucas's place. "The boy is everything Jordan said he was. Why didn't you tell us about him sooner?"

"I think you know why."

"Of course. My memory is as good as yours."

"Lucas knows who his father is," Angie said. "He's grown up with pictures and stories about him."

"But you didn't give him his father's name."

"Under the circumstances, I felt if wasn't…appropriate." No need to add that she'd wanted to hide her son from the Cooper family.

"So you wouldn't consider changing it?" The abruptness of the question startled Angie. How much had Jordan discussed with his mother on the way here?

"That would be up to Lucas," she said. "Maybe when he's older. But it would be his decision, not mine."

"I see." Meredith surveyed the dining room—the paintings on the walls, the glass-fronted hutch with its gleaming china and crystal. "I understand Jordan's allowed you to move in here," she said. "What is it you're after, Angelina? Money?"

Angie sucked back a tide of outrage. "All I want is whatever's best for Lucas," she said. "As for money, I have my own web design business. It earns enough for my needs, even here. And I'm keeping the ranch books to pay for the car I'm driving." Her chin lifted in defiance. "This was never about money, Meredith. I loved Justin, and I'd do anything to protect our son. When are you going to see that?"

Meredith drew herself up, looming over Angie in her high heels. "Well!" she huffed. *"Well!"*

Lucas bounded into the room, ending the standoff. Jordan strolled in behind him, his smile strained. Had he overheard?

"Can we eat now?" Lucas asked. "Please?"

"Why don't you go in the kitchen and ask Marta?" Jordan suggested. "If she says dinner's ready, we can sit down and let Carlos bring it in."

Lucas darted into the kitchen, leaving the grown-ups in awkward silence. "Well, Mother," Jordan asked, "what do you think?"

"Don't rush me, Jordan. It's too soon. I need time."

Meredith's voice quivered with surprising emotion. Maybe the woman had a heart, after all. But before Angie had time to ponder that thought, Lucas was back.

"It's ready!" he announced. "Come on, let's eat!"

Jordan surveyed the table over his plate of homemade pumpkin pie. All in all, the dinner could've gone worse. His mother had kept the sharp edge of her tongue in check, and Lucas had managed to get through the meal without spilling his milk or tipping out of his booster seat. He'd even remembered to say please and thank you most of the time—not a bad performance for a three-year-old.

The best thing about the day had been his mother's ready acceptance of Lucas. The documents Jordan had shown her in the car, along with the boy's resemblance to Justin, had been enough to convince her that he was indeed her grandson. It was a step in the right direction. But only a step.

Angie was an entirely different matter.

The mealtime conversation had centered on the history of the house and the famous people who'd dined here.

The topic had been safe enough, but the tension between the two women had hung like a miasma over the table.

Jordan had heard much of the earlier exchange between them. His mother was a formidable woman, but Angie had stood her ground. For that he couldn't help being proud of her.

"Would anyone else like coffee with their pie?" Meredith had slipped into her former role as hostess. A tap on the bell at the side of her plate summoned Carlos with the silver coffee service and three porcelain cups.

Lucas was getting sleepy, his eyelids drooping. Jordan was about to suggest to Angie that he be taken upstairs for a nap when a scratching sound came from the direction of the patio door.

Meredith's eyebrows shot up. "What on Earth…?"

"I'll take care of it." Carlos had finished pouring the coffee. Still balancing the tray, he hurried out of the dining room and into the parlor.

There was an ominous beat of silence. Jordan was thinking he should've gone himself when he heard the click of the opening door, followed by a loud, metallic crash and a string of Spanish curses. Tongue lolling, toenails clicking on the tiles, Rudy came galloping into the dining room.

The growing pup had put on considerable size since his arrival at the ranch. Normally well behaved, he'd probably headed to the dining room because he missed his young master—but then he'd been startled by the crash of the dropped coffee tray. As a result, he made a beeline for the table and tried to leap onto Lucas's lap.

Angie, who was closest, snatched her son to safety as the chair and booster seat toppled over. Fighting for purchase, Rudy scrabbled at the linen tablecloth, pulling part of it over the table's edge. Dishes crashed to the floor, spilling food as they shattered on the tiles.

Meredith was screaming—more in rage than in fear. "Get him! Get that horrid beast!"

By then Jordan had managed to grab Rudy's collar and haul him away from table. But the damage was done. The room reminded Jordan of a scene from a B-grade frat house movie.

Carlos hung his head. "I'm sorry, Mrs. Cooper. I opened the door a crack, the dog ran right between my legs and I dropped the tray. I'll take him out to the barn for now."

Lucas was crying. Angie held him close as Meredith rose, quivering. "I want that hideous creature gone," she said. "It's to be off the property by this time tomorrow! Get rid of it any way you have to!"

"No!" Lucas's sobs had risen to howls. "Don't take Rudy! He's my dog! He loves me!"

"Never mind," Meredith said. "We'll get you a more suitable dog, a nice golden retriever like the one your father had."

"No! I want Rudy!" Tears streamed down Lucas's cheeks.

"I'll take the dog out," Jordan said. "Carlos, you stay and help clean up. Don't worry, Lucas, Rudy's just going to the barn. He'll be safe and warm, and I'll leave him some food."

Jordan's words seemed to lend some comfort. Lucas's sobs eased. He buried his face against his mother's shoulder. "He's worn out," Angie said. "Once he's down for his nap, I'll come back and help with the cleanup. That's the least I can do."

"What about me?" Meredith dabbed a spatter of gravy

off her slacks. "I've had a trying experience, and I want to go home. Who's going to drive me?"

"I'll take you, Mother, as soon as this rascal's safely put away." Jordan kept a grip on Rudy's collar as he led the pup toward the back of the house. Minutes ago, he'd been congratulating himself on a peaceful Thanksgiving dinner. He should have known better.

By the time the Mercedes pulled into the garage, the sun was setting. Marta and Carlos had gone home after clearing away the remains of dinner, and Lucas had yet to wake from his nap.

Curled on the sofa by the glowing fire, Angie was savoring the quiet. She glanced up as Jordan came in from the patio.

"How's Lucas?" He peeled of his leather jacket and tossed it on a footstool. His hair glimmered with melting snowflakes.

"Still asleep." She remembered the fuzzy blue blanket on the bed, the small lump beneath, nestled next to Justin's teddy bear. "He was so tired, he may be down for the night. How's your mother?"

"She'll be fine." He came around the back of the couch and sat down. "We had a talk."

"Oh?"

"I made it clear that Rudy is part of the family—and so are you. And I told her that if she wanted to spend time with her grandson, she'd have to accept that."

"That sounds a bit harsh, don't you think?"

He stretched his long legs before the fire. "My mother has a good heart. But she can be stubborn. Sometimes it takes a little tough love to bring her around."

Angie stared at him, half amused. "You surprise me, Jordan Cooper, sticking up for poor Rudy like that. And sticking up for me, too. Right now I think I like you better than ever before in my life."

A smile tugged at one corner of his mouth. "That sounds like a good thing. Is it?"

Angie's pulse skittered. Jordan had taken giant steps to win her trust. Did it mean what she wanted it to mean? After all that had happened between them, dared she risk her heart to this man?

She lowered her gaze, then met his eyes. "It could be…a very good thing," she said.

Even before he leaned close and cupped her cheek with his hand, she'd sensed he was going to kiss her. But she was unprepared for the rush that slammed her body when his lips closed on hers. A moan escaped her throat as heat poured through her in a sizzling torrent. She'd wanted this, hungered for it. Heaven help her, she hadn't known how much until now.

Her mouth softened against his, lips parting, tongue seeking. With a low growl he pulled her against him, hands molding her against his chest. She clasped his head, deepening the kiss as their tongues played a tantalizing game of tag. Moisture slicked the crotch of her panties as his hand slid beneath her sweater. Skilled fingers unhooked the back of her bra. She whimpered as his palm cupped her breast, thumb stroking the nipple with a lightness that triggered spasms of need.

She wanted him so much she could hardly stand it. But things were moving too fast, spinning out of control. And there was Lucas napping upstairs, liable to wake up any second.

Summoning her will, she pulled away from him.

A questioning look flashed across his face. Then he glanced upward in sudden understanding. His breath eased out as he released her. "Rain check?"

Angie managed a shaky laugh. "Rain check. I should probably look in on Lucas again." She paused, thinking. "Nothing would make him happier than to wake up and see Rudy by his bed. Do you think—?"

"Sure. I'll go get Rudy and bring him upstairs. Let's hope the silly mutt's learned his lesson."

They rose at the same time. Angie was headed for the stairs when she realized something wasn't quite right. "Jordan, wait—" She turned her back and pulled up her sweater. "I could use a little help here."

He chuckled. "Now this is the kind of help I don't mind giving," he muttered as he fastened the back of her bra. Lingering, he let his hands slide around her rib cage to cradle the lace-clad cups. Angie closed her eyes. A purr escaped her lips as he brushed a kiss on the back of her neck.

"You're getting me in trouble," she murmured.

His laughter tickled her skin as he released her. "I sincerely hope so. Now run along. We can finish what we started later."

He picked up his jacket and strode, whistling, toward the back door. Angie raced up the stairs, her heart pounding. Was she making a fool of herself, casting aside all caution and common sense to be with Jordan again?

If the answer was yes, why did it feel so right? Was it because he'd stood up to his mother in her defense?

It didn't necessarily mean a thing, she reminded herself as she hurried down the hall toward Lucas's room. Clearly Jordan wanted a bed partner, and he could be very persuasive. The question was, did he want more?

The door to Lucas's room was slightly ajar, as she'd left it. Cracking it open a few more inches, she slipped inside. There was no sign that Lucas had stirred—but Angie noticed something as she was about to leave. His shoes, which she'd taken off and placed on the rug, were missing, and his jacket was gone from the back of the chair.

A thread of panic rose in her. Afraid to breathe, she yanked back her son's blue blanket. On the bed was a cleverly arranged line of pillows and stuffed toys.

Lucas was gone.

Ten

As she bolted down the stairs, Angie saw Jordan rushing back inside. "He's gone!" she gasped. "Lucas is gone!"

Jordan looked shaken. "I know. The dog's gone, too. I found their tracks in the snow." He grabbed his coat off the chair. "I'll go after them. Do you want to stay here and wait?"

"No, he might need me. I'm coming with you." Angie raced for the closet. While Jordan found a flashlight, Angie tugged on a thick woolen overcoat. No doubt Lucas, fearing the loss of his beloved pet, had taken Rudy and run away. The snow would make it possible to track him, thank heaven, but it was getting dark and the night was frigid. How long could a small child survive in this weather?

Together they plunged out the back door into the biting wind. Fine snowflakes blasted them like bird shot. Angie pulled the oversize coat around her, thinking of her little boy in his thin jacket. They had to find him before hypothermia set in.

"This way!" Jordan shone the light toward the corner of the barn. "Here's where I saw the tracks."

Angie stared at the ground. The prints of Lucas's sneakers and Rudy's outsize paws were already filling with snow. How long had they been gone? Too long, she realized with a sinking heart. When she'd checked on her son half an hour ago she'd been fooled by the lumpy form on the bed. At the time she'd failed to notice the missing shoes and jacket. If only she'd taken a moment for a second look.

As she followed Jordan's flashlight beam, she breathed silent prayers. By now they'd left the open gate behind and were moving fast, Angie running to keep up with Jordan's long strides. Her light slippers were cold and wet and gave her poor footing, but she struggled ahead. Every few minutes they stopped to shout Lucas's name and listen. The only answer was the chilling whistle of the wind.

Suddenly Jordan paused, cursing under his breath. Angie drew closer, trying to see the tracks through the flying snow. "What is it?" she asked.

Jordan lowered the beam, focusing the light on a narrow paw print, smaller than Rudy's. "Coyotes," he said. "Looks like maybe a pair of them. They'll run from an adult, but…"

There was no need for him to finish. Lucas was small enough to be seen as prey. And a clumsy, inexperienced pup like Rudy would be no match for a pair of hungry coyotes.

Angie's knees threatened to buckle. She willed herself to be strong. "You're faster than I am," she told Jordan. "Go on ahead. I'll follow your trail."

His hand brushed her cheek. "Don't worry. I'll find him."

"Hurry!" She watched him turn away. In the next moment he was lost in darkness and swirling snow.

Head down, Angie pushed after him.

"Lucas!" Jordan shouted into the wind, ears straining for any sign he'd been heard. If only he'd thought to bring his pistol. The boy might be able to hear a gunshot and come toward the sound. But in this weather, a voice wouldn't carry for more than a few dozen yards.

Lucas's trail had become more erratic, as if he were weakening or becoming confused. At least the dog was staying with him. Rudy's big paw prints were clear and close, the coyote tracks scattered wider as if the crafty beasts had caught up and were working up the courage to move in. Jordan paused to brush the snow off the flashlight, then raced ahead.

What if he arrived too late? Lord, what if he lost that precious little boy—his brother's only child? He'd grown to care for Lucas. Their rides in the truck and their time on the range had taken him back to his own boyhood and to the simple joys of being alive. He'd found himself looking forward to watching the boy grow up, to being there to help and guide him.

And what about Angie? Lucas's loss would destroy her. She would blame herself, just as she blamed herself for losing Justin. Even if she survived, emotionally and physically, he'd never see her again.

Jordan had to face the truth. He could no longer imagine his life without either of them.

"Lucas!" He plunged through the dark, half-blinded by snow. *"Lucas!"*

On the wind came a faint sound. A shout? No, more like a bark. Guided by his ears now, he pounded toward it.

"Lucas! Answer me!" He waited, praying for the sound of a childish voice. But he heard only more barking. With a silent prayer on his lips he pounded closer.

Two shadowy forms streaked away as he approached. There, in the beam of his flashlight, he saw Rudy. Head lowered, hackles bristling, he stood his ground, guarding something in the darkness behind him.

"Easy, boy." The pup growled at Jordan's approach but seemed to recognize his voice. Rudy's head came up. His tail twitched, then wagged.

Jordan's flashlight beam found Lucas. He was curled on his side at the base of a large creosote bush, half-sheltered by its branches.

The boy wasn't moving.

Sick with dread, Jordan flung himself to his knees and scooped the child into his arms. The small body was limp and cold, but he was still breathing. "Lucas!" Jordan shook him gently, then harder. "Lucas! Wake up!"

Lucas stirred. His eyes blinked open. "Tired…" he mumbled.

Thank God.

Stripping off his leather jacket, Jordan wrapped the boy in its warmth. "Let's go home, son," he said.

Home. Son. Strange how naturally the words came to him.

Rudy followed along as Jordan strode back the way he'd come. Angie's windblown form appeared through the driving snow. She stumbled forward with a cry as she saw him.

"He's all right, Angie, just cold." He would tell her later how close the coyotes had come and how Rudy had protected his young master.

She opened the ample overcoat she'd worn. Jordan freed Lucas from the leather jacket and passed the boy to his mother. She folded the coat around him, warming him with her body. By now he was sobbing—a good sign. Broken whimpers came from inside the coat. Impulsively, Jordan gathered them both into his arms, holding them tight against him. They stood wrapped in flying snow, breathing silent thanks for the small life that nestled between them. The moment was so poignant that he was reluctant to end it. But an impatient yip from Rudy reminded him that they needed to get back to the house.

They followed their trail toward the distant lights of the house. Angie stumbled in her thin shoes. Catching her balance, she readjusted her burden.

Jordan reached out to steady her. "You're getting tired. Let me take him."

"We're fine." Her arms tightened around her son. She'd been through a mother's hell tonight, Jordan reminded himself. Her strength amazed and humbled him. How could anyone raise children in this dangerous world where tragedies struck without warning? How could anyone have the courage to love when the risk of pain ran so high?

Was he a coward at heart? Was that why, after Justin's loss, he'd held so much back from his marriage? Was that why he'd drifted from one empty relationship to the next, his emotions safely frozen?

By the time they reached the house they were too cold and tired for conversation. Angie shed the overcoat and rushed Lucas upstairs. Jordan fed the pup and took him up to the boy's room. From Angie's bathroom, he could hear the sound of splashing water and the murmur of voices.

Going back to the kitchen, Jordan made hot cocoa

with mini marshmallows, took a cup upstairs and rapped lightly on the bathroom door. Angie opened it a few inches. Behind her he glimpsed Lucas in a tub of steaming bubbles.

Her damp face lit when she saw the cocoa. "Oh, thanks! That'll help warm him up."

"Careful, it's still hot." Jordan passed her the cup and saucer. "How's he doing?"

"Better. No sign of frostbite. But he's worn out. I'm hoping he'll sleep."

"Rudy's curled on his rug. That mutt deserves a medal. Stuck right by Lucas the whole time."

She flashed a tired smile. "See, I told you the dog was worth saving. I hope your mother's convinced of that."

"If not, she will be."

Jordan went back to the parlor and added a fresh log to the fireplace. Then he sank down on the couch to wait. There was no reason to believe Angie would come downstairs again. But he wanted her to.

And if she did, he wanted to be here, waiting.

Angie tiptoed down to the parlor. It had taken time for Lucas to fall asleep, and she hadn't wanted to leave him. But now he was deep in slumber, with Rudy keeping faithful watch beside his bed.

The empty cup and saucer had lent her an excuse to return downstairs. But she didn't expect to need it. Jordan had probably gone to bed. And, after Lucas's scare, their sizzling encounter on the sofa—and the rain check they'd promised each other—would seem little more than a distant memory.

But if he chanced to be awake she wanted to thank him. Jordan had saved her son's life tonight. Alone, there was no way she could have found Lucas in time.

In the parlor, the fire smoldered on the hearth, tongues of flame flickering among the coals. A single lamp on an end table glowed through its mica shade. In its light, Jordan sprawled on the sofa, fast asleep.

Setting the cup and saucer aside, Angie gazed down at him. He lay cushioned on his side, as if he'd nodded off while sitting and then slumped over. His hair clung to his face in damp curls; his jaw was shadowed with stubble.

A rush of tenderness swept over her. She found herself yearning to brush a kiss across his lips, imagining the taste of him, the slow stirring of his response. Tempted, she leaned toward him, then caught herself. Jordan looked exhausted. What if he didn't want to be bothered? Maybe it would be best to let him sleep.

A woolen afghan lay over the back of a chair. Shaking out the folds, Angie spread it gently over him. She was tucking it around his shoulders when he opened his eyes. His gaze was sleepy and disturbingly sexy.

"Hello," he mumbled. "How's Lucas?"

"It took him a while to settle down, but he's fine. Out for the night, I hope."

"Good." He pushed himself upright, undressing her with a heavy-lidded look. Angie felt a nervous flutter in her stomach. She'd slept with Jordan once and told herself it meant nothing. But this time, she sensed, she was risking her heart. Were things moving too fast? Maybe she'd have been wiser to stay in her room.

"Sit down, Angie," he said as if reading her. "You've been through a hell of a time. Put your feet up and rest."

"That sounds like the best advice I've heard all night."

As she sank into the leather cushions, he shifted to give her more room and shoved the ottoman over to support her feet.

"Better?"

She answered with a nod and a little sigh.

"Coffee? I can make you some."

"No, thanks. It'll just keep me awake."

One dark eyebrow twitched upward. What had he read into that last remark? Jordan wouldn't push her, she knew. He had too much male pride for that. Whatever happened—or didn't happen—would be her decision.

Rising, he moved to the ottoman and lifted her feet in his hands. Only then did Angie realize that she was still wearing the thin, wet slippers that had trudged through the snow.

Gently, he peeled off the soggy shoes and shook his head. "Poor feet. They're like lumps of ice. Wait here. I'll be right back."

He left the room and returned a moment later with a washcloth, a towel and a mysterious-looking jar. Sitting again, he cradled Angie's bare feet on the towel in his lap. His eyes held a mischievous twinkle. "Just lean back and enjoy this," he said.

Angie's eyes closed as Jordan sponged her chilled feet and rubbed them dry. Her breath eased out in a whispered moan. The cloth was damp, warm and soft, the sensation so sweet it almost brought her to tears. Had anyone, in her whole life, ever done such a thing for her?

"You learned this from the devil, along with that shoulder massage, didn't you?" she joked, making light of what she felt.

He flashed her a grin. "Sure. In exchange for my soul."

"I bet you do this for all the ladies."

"Only the ones with frozen feet." He opened the jar. The silky cream he rubbed into her skin had a tingle and smelled of sandalwood. His powerful fingers massaged the arches and balls of her feet, awakening sparks of pleasure that shimmered upward along her calves, into her thighs and…

Angie groaned as the heat rose and curled inside her. Her senses simmered, melting like butter over a flame. "This is decadent," she murmured. "You're a naughty man, Jordan Cooper."

"You don't know the half of it." His eyes narrowed in the lamplight, flashing a half-hidden challenge. His fingers continued their slow torment. Waves of arousal rippled up her legs. She shuddered with need. How long was the man going to tease her like this?

"I think I'd like to…" she whispered.

"Like to what?"

"To…know the other half…"

With a rough laugh, he rose and swept her up in his arms. Carrying her like a child, he strode down the hall to his bedroom. Angie almost expected to be flung onto the mattress, but he stopped at the side of the bed and gently lowered her feet to the floor. His kiss was long and warm and deep—so deep that she felt the burn of it all the way to the soles of her bare feet.

Through his clothes she could feel the contours of his broad chest, his muscled belly and the strain of his jutting sex. Her hand crept down to tug at the zipper pull.

"Tell me what you want, Angie." His voice was a velvety growl.

Her fingers opened the zipper and found the slit in his briefs. "This…" Her fingertip stroked the solid length of his shaft. A quiver passed through his body.

"Tell me. Let me hear you say it."

"I want you, Jordan." Had she ever been surer of anything in her life? "I want you inside me."

He took seconds to drop his clothes and add protection. Then his hands jerked her slacks and panties off her hips.

As they pooled around her ankles he clasped her rump, lifted her upward and slid her onto his iron-hard length.

Angie gasped as he entered her. Unbidden, her bare legs wrapped around his hips, binding him close, and her arms wrapped around his neck. A whimper stirred her throat as his thrusts began, driving upward, pushing into her high and hard. A storm of sensations surged through her body. She found herself wanting to move with him, but gravity was working against her. It was all she could do to hang on and enjoy the wild ride.

"Jordan—" she whispered.

As if sensing what she needed, he moved against the side of the mattress and eased down onto his back, with her thighs straddling his hips and his sex deep inside her.

"I'm all yours, lady," he muttered.

"Oh…" Her breath emerged as a moan. Driven by instinct she pushed against him, deepening his thrust. With every move, her senses exploded, pounding, throbbing. Her body pulsed, clenching around his shaft as everything shattered in one glorious burst. She slumped over him, her tension drained away in a wash of sweet gratitude.

He drew her close, kissing her and cradling her in his arms. "You're a bit of a naughty girl yourself," he whispered. "Just let me finish here."

With their bodies still joined, he rolled over on top of her. One last gliding thrust took him deep. He came with a groan and a shudder. Angie held him tight, feeling his powerful body relax in her arms. If only they could stay like this, she thought, shut away from the world, warm and close and at peace. But she knew better than to believe the moment would last.

A laugh rumbled in his throat as he slid off her and stretched out on his back. "Lord, Angie, you'll be the death of me," he muttered.

"I'd better go." She sat up and began groping for her clothes.

"Don't." His hand closed around her wrists. "I know you'll be wanting to get back to Lucas, but there's time. Stay a little longer."

"What if I go to sleep?"

"I know you, Angie. As long as Lucas is upstairs, you won't let yourself nod off. And I won't keep you long. I just don't want to let you go yet."

He curled on his side and drew her into the warm hollow next to his body. They lay quietly, his breath stirring her hair. Heaven, she thought. But she couldn't let herself believe it would last.

"How long has it been since anyone's taken care of you, Angie?" he asked.

His question caught her by surprise. She shook her head. "My parents died when I was sixteen. Even when they were alive, they were working so hard to keep food in our bellies that I was pretty much on my own."

"So your answer is, not for a very long time?"

When had this conversation become so serious? "There was Justin, of course," she ventured.

"Of course." He pulled her closer into the curve of his body. "Did he take care of you?"

Angie sighed. "You know he was good to me. But somehow, I always seemed to be the one looking after him— getting him places on time, making sure he remembered things like birthdays. Justin was so sweet, so charming. It was as if he didn't feel the need to account for himself...."

Her voice trailed off as she sensed his silence and realized what she'd just said.

"I'm sorry," she added, flustered. "What an awful thing for me to say. Your brother was kind and generous."

"Don't apologize for speaking the truth. I did my own

share of looking after my brother." His throat moved against her hair as he swallowed. "What I'm trying to say is there's no need for you to wear yourself out with work and worry. I know you value your independence, but I can easily take care of you and Lucas. I want to, Angie. To tell the truth, I need to."

"But you take care of us already. You've given us this beautiful place to stay, good food, a reliable car…." Angie broke off as a realization struck her.

"You said you *needed* to take care of us? Why, Jordan?"

"Does there have to be a reason? Lucas is my brother's son. And you're his mother. If you'd let me, there's so much I could offer the two of you—travel all over the world, your own investments for the future, even your own home if you wanted one. And I could open doors, introduce you to—"

"Stop it." Angie sat bolt upright, trembling. "Have you forgotten something?"

He stared up at her, his expression veiled in shadow, as she continued.

"Justin would still be here if it weren't for me. But he died because it was my birthday, and he wanted to fly out to be with me. As if that weren't enough, I kept Justin's son, his own flesh and blood, hidden from your family for four years."

Angie could feel her fragile control crumbling. She swung her feet to the floor and snatched up what she could find of her clothes, clutching them in front of her.

"Take care of me? Why would you want to? You and your mother have every reason to hate me!" She took a deep breath, feeling how perilously close she was to tears. "Sometimes I hate myself," she whispered. "And that's why I can't accept anything more from you. Anything at all." Gathering her clothes again, she headed for the door. This time, he didn't stop her.

Eleven

Jordan punched his pillow as Angie's retreating footsteps pattered into silence. Part of him wanted to run after her, but what could he say? There was no way he could convince her that she was wrong without telling her who was *really* to blame for Justin's death. Still, he hated to think of the broken look in her eyes when she'd left. He never should have let her start on in the topic in the first place. All he'd really wanted was to keep her beside him in his bed long enough to lose himself inside her again. But one thing had led to another. Now here they were, at odds again. He had no one to blame but himself.

He'd claimed to have looked after his happy-go-lucky brother, and he had. What he hadn't told her was how, in the end, he'd failed. When Justin had needed him most, he hadn't been there. Worse, he'd driven his brother away— sent him off angry and hurt and rushing headlong into disaster.

Would Angie have come to his bed tonight if she'd known the full story?

But why even wonder? If she'd known, he was certain she wouldn't have come within a hundred miles of him.

Wide awake now, he rolled onto his back and lay staring up at the dark *vigas* that crossed the whitewashed ceiling. With any other woman, he'd have shrugged off the conflict, kissed her goodbye and moved on. But Angie wasn't just any woman. She and her son had become a vital part of his life, bringing out a tender protectiveness he hadn't even known he possessed. He didn't want to lose them. He didn't want to lose *her*.

Angie had shouldered the entire blame for Justin's death. The truth would lighten her burden. It would also tarnish Justin—and him—in her eyes forever.

But the question was not *whether* to tell Angie. It was when and how. Jordan had been living a lie for four long years. Sooner or later that lie was bound to blow up in his face.

Angie had the right to know what had sent Justin's plane crashing into that Utah mountain. As the only one who knew the full story, it would be up to Jordan to tell her. But not yet, he resolved. Until Lucas's name was on the family trust as Justin's heir, he couldn't risk causing Angie to take her son and disappear from his life.

It was that damned balancing act again.

He needed to take action before something else went wrong. Maybe it would be a good idea to spend a few days at his condo in town. He could use some time to catch up on work at the office. More important, he could have the papers drawn up for the change to the trust and maybe even persuade his mother to sign them.

The more Jordan thought about the idea, the better it sounded. After tonight's blistering encounter, Angie would probably welcome a break from him. And he could use some quiet time, too. Maybe without the distraction of wanting her every blasted minute of the day, he'd be able to get his head straight.

He would leave tomorrow at first light.

Back in her room, Angie dropped her clothes on a chair and slipped into her nightgown. Peeking in Lucas's door, she found her son still fast asleep. Tiptoeing closer, she brushed a kiss across his forehead. His skin was cool, his breathing effortless. No fever. Thank heaven for small miracles, for Rudy…and for Jordan.

A warm flush crept over her skin as she remembered her behavior in Jordan's bed. *Shameless*—there was no better word to describe it. Every part of her had craved him, and she'd taken all she could.

Things had been wonderful until Jordan had opened his mouth.

He'd talked about taking care of her. What on Earth was that supposed to mean? It couldn't have been a marriage proposal. Jordan had never led her to believe he loved her.

Earlier, when she'd told him she wouldn't be his mistress, he'd dismissed the notion as Victorian blather. But what else could the man have in mind? He may not have meant for his gifts to come across as payment for her favors in bed, but that was certainly how it seemed! The SUV had come right after their first night together, and now after a second encounter, he was offering to send her on expensive trips and set up investment accounts for her. He could call it what he liked, but it was an arrangement as old as human history, and she wanted no part of it!

So what did she want? She wanted to amount to something, to earn her own money, further her education, marry a good man who valued and respected her and give Lucas the chance to grow up in a loving home with brothers and sisters.

The longer she remained here on Jordan's charity, the less likely she'd be to realize her own goals. If she gave in to what he wanted, she'd be no better than a house pet, living off Jordan's money until he wearied of her and moved on to someone else.

Then what would she be?

And what about her son?

Her mind was fogging over. Exhausted, she walked back to her room, sank into bed and pulled the quilt up to her ears. She needed a day away from the ranch. And she needed a friendly ear. Tomorrow she would take Lucas, drive into town and spend some time with Raquel. A dose of her cousin's warm wisdom could be just the right medicine for her troubled heart.

Still making plans, she tumbled into sleep.

Angie woke the next morning to find a folded note tucked under her door.

Gone into town for a few days. You have my cell. I'll be in touch. J.

That was all. No details. No mention of last night. No word of affection. It was so damnably like Jordan that she wanted to grind her teeth.

Tossing the note into the wastebasket, she went to wake her son. Thank heaven she had her own plans. Maybe she could even put Jordan out of her mind for a few hours.

After a late breakfast and a quick game of "fetch" with Rudy, she bundled Lucas into his car seat and set out for downtown Santa Fe. Last night's storm had swept eastward, leaving a light snow that glittered in the morning sunlight. The Sangre de Cristo Mountains rose diamond white against a sky of dazzling turquoise.

By now the stores would have their Christmas displays up. Lucas would enjoy that. They could wander around the Plaza and then drive somewhere for two-dollar burgers and root beer. She could call her cousin from the restaurant. That way they wouldn't be showing up at Raquel's unannounced and hungry.

By 11:00 they'd parked the car and were taking in the lights and decorations around the Plaza. Lucas's eyes were wide with wonder. Last year he'd been too young to understand or remember much about Christmas. This year he noticed everything. He'd be chattering about it all the way home.

By the time they'd strolled in and out of uncounted shops, exclaiming over toys and sampling free treats, Angie was getting tired. Lucas whined when she announced it was time to go back to the car but cheered up at the mention of a kiddie meal. They were headed back around the Plaza when she heard a reedy male voice behind her.

"Angie Montoya! What a small world!"

She turned to see a lanky, bespectacled man grinning down at her. Awkward seconds ticked by before she remembered him. It was Trevor Wilkins, Justin's old friend who'd cornered her at Jordan's party.

"I've been hoping I'd see you again," he said. "The last time we met I'd had a few drinks. If I crossed the line and made you uncomfortable, I'm sorry. Will you accept my apology?"

"Of course." Angie gave him a smile. True, he'd been mildly obnoxious. But until now she hadn't given his behavior—or him—a second thought.

His gaze fell on Lucas. "So this is your son. I can see a lot of Justin in him."

"Everyone seems to." Angie was aware of Lucas tugging at her hand. "Now, if you'll excuse us, we were just leaving to get some lunch at Burger Box."

"Oh?" Trevor brightened. "Then why not have lunch with me? I have a table reserved at *La Fonda*. I'd love to treat the two of you."

"Oh, that's kind of you, but I couldn't impose." *La Fonda,* the old hotel on the Plaza, was a Santa Fe legend. Its *La Plazuela* dining room was way out of Angie's price range.

"Give me one good reason why not," Trevor argued.

"Have you ever eaten in a nice restaurant with a three-year-old?"

"I have nephews. Come on, don't worry about it. Just lunch. No strings attached."

Angie sighed. Trevor had been Justin's good friend, and she didn't want to offend him. There was no graceful way to refuse. "All right," she said. "But don't say I didn't warn you."

It was barely noon, but the elegant 1920s dining room was already filling up. Trevor's table was in a quiet corner. Angie plotted a line to the nearest door. With luck Lucas would behave. But he was getting cranky, and the only way to deal with a three-year-old meltdown was a fast exit.

The server brought a booster seat along with the menus. "I want a hamburger," Lucas said.

Trevor glanced up from his menu. "They do a good burger here. But it's pretty big."

"In that case, we'll split it," Angie said. "Nothing but meat on Lucas's half, everything on mine. Can they do that?"

It seemed they could. The server took their orders and left them to make small talk. Angie was seated next to the wall with a view of the rest of the dining room. Trevor sat across from her, his back to the other tables. Thus he didn't notice the couple who walked into the restaurant—the tall handsome man dressed in a sweater and tweed jacket, the older woman, her crimson pantsuit and silver hair impeccable.

Angie shrank in her chair as Jordan and his mother took their seats.

Jordan had spotted Angie at once. He opened the menu, doing his best to ignore her. There was no reason to get upset, he told himself. Angie was a free woman. But a rendezvous with Trevor Wilkins? The sight of her and Lucas at Trevor's table had hit him like a kick in the gut.

At least his mother was facing away from them. Jordan had brought Meredith here, to her favorite restaurant, in the hope of easing her toward accepting Angie and Lucas. So far she'd seemed agreeable. But seeing Angie with another man could set off an avalanche of suspicion.

Not that Trevor was a bad sort. He'd inherited his father's real estate agency and often did business with Jordan's firm. Maybe he was just what Angie needed—decent, steady, dependable…and boring.

Had Angie called Trevor when she'd found herself free for the day? That made sense. But if this was some kind of romantic liaison, why had she brought Lucas along? Damn it, these questions were driving him crazy.

He had no right to be jealous. Angie may have shared his bed, but she wasn't wearing his ring. He had no claim on her.

And he wasn't the jealous type. Even his ex-wife's affair had left him cold—he'd expected it to happen and hadn't much cared.

Jordan could only remember feeling jealousy at one period in his life. That was while his brother was engaged to Angie Montoya. He'd pushed his emotions aside then, and he could do it now.

Focusing on the menu, Jordan forced himself to make pleasant conversation with his mother. Maybe if he kept her distracted, she wouldn't turn around and see what was right in his line of vision.

Lucas scowled at the plate in front of him. "This isn't my hamburger. My hamburger comes in a clown box."

Angie sighed. "This hamburger is special, Lucas. See, you have half and I have half. It's yummy. Taste it."

"No." Lucas shook his head. "I don't like it."

"How do you know you don't like it? You haven't even tried it." Trevor's adult logic wasn't helping.

"I get a toy with my hamburger. I want a toy!"

People at nearby tables were glancing around. "Lucas, that's enough!" Angie hissed. "One more word and we're out of here."

"I want a toy!" Lucas's voice rose to a full-decibel three-year-old whine. *"I...want...a...TOY!"*

With everyone in the restaurant staring, Angie snatched up her son and dashed for the nearest exit.

"And then what happened, *querida?*" Raquel added a dollop of cream to her coffee.

"Trevor came after me with my purse. I apologized to him in the lobby and left." Angie forced herself to nibble a fresh cinnamon *churro* dusted with sugar.

"So Jordan and his mother saw you."

"Everybody saw us! I've never been so embarrassed in my life."

"And there you were with Trevor." Raquel chuckled. "Why should I watch the *telenovelas* when I've got my crazy little cousin?"

"It isn't funny, Raquel. For all I know, Jordan's mother thinks Trevor and I are conspiring to rob her family blind. Heavens, I scarcely know the man!"

"So you don't plan on dating him? He seems to like you—and I hear he's got money."

Angie shook her head. "It doesn't matter. After today, I can't imagine Trevor would want to see me again."

"And Jordan?"

Angie's gaze flickered downward. Through the window of Raquel's cheerful kitchen came the shouts of children playing tag in the patio.

Raquel's sharp eyes took on a knowing expression. "Don't tell me it happened again! *Chica,* what do you think you're doing?"

Angie shrugged, fighting tears. "I don't know. I don't understand him. That's why I'm here."

"Do you love him?" Raquel asked gently.

"I don't know. Jordan isn't an easy man to love."

"Does he love you?"

"He's never said so. Only that he wants to take care of me and Lucas. What's that supposed to mean? What would make a man say something like that?"

Raquel's brows furrowed above her dark eyes. "Guilt, maybe?"

"Guilt?" Angie felt the word slam into her. "You mean guilt over Justin's death? But the crash wasn't Jordan's fault. It was mine."

"That's what you've always assumed." Raquel refilled

Angie's cup with hot black coffee. "How much do you know about the accident? Tell me what you remember."

Angie sipped her coffee. She'd done her best to bury the events leading to Justin's plane crash. It wouldn't be easy, bringing them to light again.

"Justin and Jordan had been at odds over our engagement," she began. "They were barely speaking to each other. As a Christmas gift, their parents booked them a ski trip in Park City, Utah."

"Hoping that a nice vacation would bring the boys back together," Raquel finished the thought.

"Jordan had some business and couldn't get away until late January. My birthday was coming up on the twenty-third. Justin promised he'd be back to celebrate with me. The forecast was for clear weather all week, so they decided to save time and take Justin's plane to the local airport in Heber City. If only..."

Angie gulped back tears. She'd been over those *ifs* so many times. If only they'd flown commercial to Salt Lake City. If only they'd gone earlier, or later. If only she hadn't been so set on having Justin back in town for her birthday. If only...

"Don't, *querida*." Raquel laid a hand on her arm. "You can't go back and change things. Just tell me the rest of the story."

"There's not much left to tell. On the night of the twenty-second, Justin took a cab to the airport alone, took off in his plane around midnight and crashed a few minutes later. That's all I know."

"So you don't know what caused the crash?"

"The weather was clear, with a full moon. The plane was new, and Justin was certified for instrument flying at night. There shouldn't have been a problem."

"Why did he decide to go back alone, late at night? Have you ever asked Jordan?"

"It's not something either of us wants to talk about. Most likely they weren't getting along. Or maybe Jordan just wanted to stay longer. Maybe he'd met someone." The cup trembled in Angie's hand. "I've never brought it up—never wanted to."

"What about the accident report? Did you ever ask to see it?"

"Why would I? Justin was dead. Knowing how it happened wouldn't bring him back. And his family didn't want any part of me."

Rising, Angie carried her cup to the window. From there she could see her son on the patio, gleefully flinging snowballs with Ramon.

In a few years Lucas would be old enough to ask questions about his father's death. Raquel was right. She needed more information.

"I don't know where to start," she said. "The accident report would've been filed in Utah, not here in New Mexico. Even if I found the right person to ask, why should they give me access to it?"

"They might not," Raquel said. "But I'm betting Victor could get it for you."

"Oh…that's right!" Angie had forgotten that Raquel's younger brother, Victor, was a police officer here in Santa Fe. He might have the authority to request information.

"I'll call him for you." Raquel had flipped open her cell phone and was already punching in the number. Angie heard the faint ring. Raquel made a thumbs-up sign as the call was answered.

"Victor? Listen, Cousin Angie is with me. She needs a little favor, and I'm hoping you can help her out. Here, I'll put her on."

* * *

The phone call ended with Victor's promise to call Angie back when he had more information. An hour later Angie was on the road, with Lucas asleep in his car seat. She drove with her eyes fixed on the road, but her mind was whirling like a carousel.

Had she done the right thing, prying into the circumstances of Justin's plane crash? Part of her wanted to believe Raquel—that it needed to be done. But she'd spent four years building a wall against the pain of Justin's loss. How could she tear down that wall and expose herself to more hurt?

Did she really want to know why Justin had taken off in the dead of night and flown straight into a mountain? Did she want to know why Jordan had stayed behind?

Was she strong enough to face the truth?

Of course, the accident report wouldn't give her the whole picture. Sooner or later, she knew, she would have to confront Jordan to get his account. But that was a conversation they'd need to have in person, which meant waiting until he came back.

By the time she arrived at the ranch Angie was worn out. But she'd promised to get some design suggestions to a client by the end of the day. Switching on her computer, she went to work.

Forty-five minutes later her cell phone rang. Her pulse rocketed. Would it be Jordan? Would he give her a chance to explain what he'd seen in the restaurant today?

But the caller wasn't Jordan. It was Trevor, with a follow-up to their disastrous lunch. "I'd be happy to give you a rain check," he said. "How about dinner one of these nights—without your son?"

Angie sighed. "As I told you, Trevor, Lucas is the man

in my life right now. If you want to take me out alone, you're welcome to ask again in about fifteen years."

Trevor took the rejection decently. Afterward, the phone lay quiet on Angie's desk. Its silence seemed to mock her. Jordan's note had said he'd be in touch. But that was before the fiasco at the restaurant.

Blast the man, why didn't he call? She needed to hear his voice. She needed a chance to clear up what had happened today. But as the hours passed, the leaden certainty grew that she wasn't going to hear from him. True, she had his cell phone number. But calling him was out of the question. If Jordan wasn't alone, she didn't want to know.

"Do you love him?" Raquel's question taunted her. For a plethora of reasons, Jordan Cooper was the last man she should love. But right now the thought of being separated from him by a silly misunderstanding had her almost frantic.

Did she love him?

She was in no condition to answer that question.

She went through the motions of dinner and getting Lucas ready for bed. Once he was down, she curled in front of the big-screen TV in the den, watching mindless programs until she was too drowsy to keep her eyes open. Only then did she drag herself up the stairs, fall into bed and sink into merciful sleep.

The ringing phone woke her. Sunlight was streaming into the room. What time was it?

Her groping fingers found the phone on the nightstand and pressed the answer button. Would it be Jordan?

"Hullo?" she muttered.

"Angie, this is Victor."

Her heart dropped. She sat up. "Did you find something?"

"I have the faxed report from Utah right here." His

voice sounded crisply professional. "The plane was pretty smashed up, as you can imagine."

"Yes, I'm sure." Angie felt vaguely ill.

"Just one thing appeared to have caused the crash. According to the coroner's report, when they checked the pilot's blood the alcohol level was more than twice the legal limit."

Angie stifled a groan. "You mean to say Justin had been drinking?"

"That's right. The man was too drunk to walk a straight line, let alone fly a plane."

Twelve

Angie huddled on the edge of the bed. Her crossed arms gripped her shoulders as if she were trying to keep herself from flying apart.

For almost four years she'd blamed herself for Justin's death. She'd let others blame her, too. Why hadn't anyone told her the truth?

Justin's plane had crashed because he'd taken off in the middle of the night staggering, stupid drunk.

Who else would have known? Jordan, certainly. He'd been in Utah when the accident happened. But it did make some sense that he'd keep the truth to himself, wanting to spare his parents the pain of knowing how their son died.

Had he also wanted to spare her from thinking badly of Justin? Maybe so. And yet she still wished he'd told her the truth. At least then some of the awful burden of guilt would have lifted from her shoulders.

Rising, she opened the door into her son's adjoining bedroom. Lucas was up and gone. The aromas from downstairs told her she'd find him in the kitchen, feasting on Marta's pancakes.

Justin's photograph smiled at her from the nightstand. As she studied the much-loved face with its confident grin, a cold bitterness welled up inside her.

In the years since his death, she'd started to forget Justin's flaws. When she spoke of him to Lucas, she only told the good stories—the ones that painted Justin in the best light. But now she was reminded of the other side of his character. Yes, he had been handsome, charming, generous and sweet. But he'd also been impulsive, irresponsible and frustratingly reckless.

How could you? The silent whisper rose from the depths of her loss. *How could you have done this to me... to Lucas...to all the people who loved you?*

Turning away, she closed the door. Someday she would have to tell Lucas the truth about the father he idolized. But not for years. Not until he was old enough to understand. Jordan, however, was another matter.

How Justin had died was just one piece of the puzzle. What she needed to know was why he'd taken off drunk and why he'd been drinking in the first place. Only Jordan would have the answers to her questions.

Should she confront him on sight, demanding to know everything? That might not be the wisest approach. Jordan could close up or give her an evasive answer. Watching and waiting might teach her more about his motives and what he'd kept hidden. But being around him would already be difficult enough after the way she'd fallen into his arms and then run away. She wondered if he felt the same way—awkward and uncertain—and if that was why he hadn't called.

Did she love him?

The question haunted her. She couldn't deny she had feelings for Jordan. But how could she love the man who'd kept such a terrible secret from her? Jordan had let his family blame her for Justin's death. He'd let her blame herself—when all the time he'd known the truth.

Even if she did love him, how could she forgive him?

Jordan showed up Monday afternoon after a three-day absence. Angie and Lucas were in the den watching TV when he walked in looking red-eyed and weary, as if he'd barely slept.

Had someone been keeping him awake at night? But what did it matter? Jordan was a free man. She had no claim on him.

"Uncle Jordan!" With a squeal of joy, Lucas bounded across the room to fling himself against Jordan's legs. Jordan ruffled the boy's hair, but his questioning gaze remained on Angie.

She willed her expression to freeze, revealing nothing as she switched off the TV.

"Mama and I taught Rudy to beg," Lucas said. "Do you want to see? I can get Rudy. He's outside."

"In just a second." Jordan sounded distracted, Angie thought. And he looked troubled.

"I brought Rudy a present to thank him for saving you." Jordan reached into his jacket and brought out a small bag bearing the logo of an exclusive pet store. "You can open it for him," he told Lucas.

"Wow!" Lucas drew out an elegant red leather collar with a silver tag attached to a metal ring. "It's got writing on it. I can read the numbers—I learned how in my school. What else does it say?"

Jordan crouched, bringing him to eye level with Lucas. "This is Rudy's name. And this is the phone number of the ranch. Now if he gets lost or runs away, the person who finds him can call us."

"Rudy won't run away. He loves me."

"Yes, he does. And this tag will help people know he's your dog. Oh, wait, there's something else. Can you reach in this pocket and find it?"

Lucas thrust his hand into Jordan's jacket. His eyes lit as he pulled out a braided leather leash, red to match the collar.

"Now you can walk Rudy in style," Jordan said, rising.

"Can we put the collar on him now?"

"Sure. Get your coat."

"It's right here." Lucas pulled on the jacket he'd flung over the chair earlier. Jordan's eyes met Angie's as the two of them went out. *We need to talk,* his expression said.

Fueled by nervous energy, Angie rose and began tidying the den, fluffing the pillows, straightening the rugs, picking up stray cups and carrying them to the kitchen. She'd just witnessed how the bond was growing between Lucas and Jordan. Was it a good thing, or was her precious son headed for heartbreak?

And what about her own heart? Maybe it would have been better if they'd never agreed to come here.

Jordan returned a few minutes later, alone. "Carlos is watching Lucas," he said. "It's sunny out. What do you say we go for a walk?"

Angie had hung her coat in the entry closet. She put it on, and they set out along the same trail they'd taken with the horses. An early winter thaw had moved in, melting the snow on the path. A flock of blackbirds swooped in elegant tracery against the azure sky.

They walked in silence for a few moments, Jordan's hands thrust into his pockets, Angie's eyes on the ground. Although the accident report had filled her thoughts for the past few days, seeing Jordan had reminded her of one more issue that stood between them—one that needed to be laid to rest. At last Angie spoke.

"Whatever you think you saw between me and Trevor, it was nothing. We ran into him in the Plaza, and he offered to treat us to lunch. After Lucas's meltdown we went our separate ways. End of story—except for a phone call that went nowhere."

Jordan exhaled. "You don't owe me an explanation, Angie. You're free to see anyone you like. But just so you'll know, I ran into Trevor the next day. He told me what happened. As you said, end of story."

Angie released a nervous laugh. "What a fiasco—especially when I spotted you with your mother."

"Unfortunately, my mother didn't think it was funny."

"Oh?" Angie felt a shiver of premonition. "Is that why you're looking so serious?"

He walked on for a few steps. The sun had vanished behind a cloud. The light breeze had taken on a chill.

"You know about my plan to get Lucas named as Justin's heir to the trust," he said.

"Of course."

"This weekend, while I was in town, I had our family lawyer draw up the paperwork to make the change. Since my mother had met Lucas and seemed to accept him, I was hoping I could get her signature. She appeared to be leaning that way—until she saw you with Trevor in the restaurant."

"Oh, no!" Angie halted in her tracks. "I can just imagine—"

"Can you? My mother has a suspicious nature, and she's very protective of her family. Her new theory is that you and your so-called boyfriend are using Lucas to get your hands on Justin's inheritance."

"But that's so wrong! If you feel that Lucas should be named Justin's heir then that's up to you, but for myself, I wouldn't take a penny of Justin's money! As for poor, innocent Trevor—"

"Hush, Angie." He caught her hands, imprisoning them in his powerful fingers. "You don't have to convince me. You're one of the most trustworthy souls I've ever known. I've said as much to my mother. But she's a stubborn woman, and once she sets her mind…"

He shook his head, releasing Angie's hands. "There's something else. Something I shouldn't even tell you, but you need to know."

"What's that?" Was he finally going to come clean about Justin's death?

"This morning my mother gave me an ultimatum. She told me that she'd sign the trust document on one condition—that you accept a generous check, give up all parental rights and let her adopt Lucas."

Angie felt the blood draining from her face. The ground under her feet had turned to quicksand. "No!" The word exploded like a gunshot. "So help me God, I'd never give him up! Not for all the money in the world!"

"That's pretty much what I told her—before I walked out."

"Why does it all have to be about money?" She was trembling, barely able to stand. "Tell me that if you're so smart, Jordan Cooper!"

"It isn't about money. It's about family. And whether my mother likes it or not, you and Lucas have become part of mine. I'll do whatever it takes to keep you both." He yanked her close and kissed her hard.

Caught by surprise, Angie resisted for the space of a heartbeat. Then her mouth responded to his demanding lips. Her arms slid around his neck, pulling him closer as their bodies blended.

Did she love him? This impossible man?

Lord help her, what was she going to do now?

He released her, his gaze concerned. Was there worse news to come?

"I've been racking my brain for a way to protect Lucas and ensure his place," he said. "There's one thing we could do—a sort of end run, if you will."

"Tell me."

He took a deep breath before he spoke. "You and I could get married, and I could adopt Lucas. He wouldn't be Justin's heir, but he'd be mine. In the end it would work out pretty much the same."

Angie stared at him, thunderstruck. Was this Jordan's idea of a proposal? What made him think she'd go along with such a calculating arrangement?

"I'd like to hope Lucas would be pleased," Jordan said.

Still reeling, Angie found her voice. "But you don't love me. I know you don't."

"I care for you, Angie. I want the best for you and Lucas. Isn't that enough?"

At least he hadn't lied. But was it enough? How could it be?

"And what about your mother?" she asked.

"She'd be upset at first. But she'd get used to the idea in time. As for you, you'd have the finest life money could buy—clothes, cars, travel, security…"

"Like your first wife?"

Shock flashed, then his eyes went cold. "That's a low blow, Angie."

"Is it?" She flung the words at him. "And you don't think it's a low blow to offer me a list of *things,* as if that was ever what I wanted? At least Justin loved me!"

His expression had gone rigid. Unable to face him any longer, Angie wheeled and raced back up the path toward the house.

Jordan watched her go, the wind fluttering her black hair as she fled. Fled from him.

Damn it, he'd meant well, asking Angie to marry him. He was desperate to do right by her and by his brother's son. But the words had come out all wrong. If she thought he was the world's biggest jackass he could hardly blame her.

He knew what she'd wanted to hear. She'd wanted him to say that he loved her—three words that had always stuck in his throat. If love was wanting to be with her, wanting to cherish and protect her, wanting to make a family with her and Lucas, then yes, he did love Angie.

But as long as past secrets lay between them, the words would have the ring of hypocrisy. Better not to say them at all than to have her fling them back in his face one day.

The full story of Justin's death was known only to him. As long as he kept it locked inside, Justin's shining memory would be safe. Let it out, and the truth would seep like venom through his family. No one would be immune—not his mother, not Angie, not even Lucas.

On the drive home, he'd weighed the wisdom of sharing his secret with Angie. By the time he'd turned the car into the ranch gate, he'd concluded that he couldn't take the risk.

Years ago he'd committed a Chinese proverb to memory—*A man is a slave to what he says and a master of what he keeps to himself.* He'd recalled that proverb today. Tell the story just once and the consequences would spread like wildfire, beyond his control.

There was no other way. He would have to bury the

truth forever. It would cease to exist, except in the black depths of his heart where he hid his own guilt from those who needed him.

He hadn't given up on Angie. If he could convince her to marry him, he would do his best to be a loving husband, and a caring father.

But even then, the secret would never set him free.

Dinner had been an ordeal. Lucas had kept up an animated chat with Jordan while Angie picked at her grilled chicken. She'd been relieved when the meal ended and she could flee upstairs to get her son ready for bed.

While the tub filled with bubbles and warm water, she laid out clean pajamas and tomorrow's school clothes. Lucas played in the bath until she was ready to wash his hair.

"Did Rudy like his new collar and leash?" she asked, lathering the baby shampoo.

"He wagged his tail a lot." Lucas tilted his head back so she could rinse his hair. "Can we live here forever, Mama?" he asked.

Pain jerked around Angie's heart. Since her clash with Jordan she'd been weighing her options. None of them were good, but after all that had happened here how could she not plan to leave?

"Forever's a long time, Lucas," she said. "Sometimes things have to change."

"Why?" He looked ready to burst into tears. "I want this to be our home. I want Uncle Jordan to be my new daddy."

Angie's throat tightened. "We'll talk about that later," she said, boosting her son onto the mat. He was quiet while she toweled him dry. But she knew she wasn't in the clear when, dressed in his pajamas, Lucas knelt on the rug to say his prayers.

"Bless my mama," he said. "Bless Rudy. Bless Uncle Jordan that he'll want to be my daddy. Bless us that we can live here forever. Amen." He looked up with a little smile that suggested everything was well in hand. "Good night, Mama."

"Good night, my big boy." Angie blinked back tears as she tucked the quilt around him. "I'll let Rudy in for you."

The pup was waiting by the outside door. When Angie let him in, he trotted to his usual place on the rug and lay down. Needing a quiet moment, she closed the door behind her and stepped out onto the balcony.

The air was chilly through her thin sweater but the twilight stillness was welcome. She leaned on the wrought-iron railing, watching shadows darken in the patio below. Beyond the walls, snow-covered mountains glowed crimson in the last rays of sunset, invoking the name the Spanish padres had given them—*Sangre de Cristo,* Blood of Christ.

Angie closed her eyes and filled her lungs with the cool freshness. Her ears caught the twitter of sparrows and the distant, mournful wail of a coyote.

As her emotions welled, a single tear trickled down her cheek. She had tried not to love this place, but she'd failed. She loved it, just as Lucas did. And she loved the troubled man who called it home.

Not that loving Jordan made things any easier. If she weren't in love with him, she might be able to endure a sham marriage for Lucas's sake. But love would open her to a world of hurt. Could she bear it day after day, knowing Jordan had married her only out of duty?

But how could she let her own feelings matter when Lucas's happiness was at stake? He wanted to grow up here on the ranch, with Jordan as his father. And it was within her power to make it happen. How could she deny her beloved child what he'd prayed for?

Angie heard the scrape of a boot on the tiles. Before she could turn around, a soft blanket wrapped her from behind. "It's cold out here," Jordan said. "I don't want you catching a chill."

Angie snuggled into the woolen warmth. It was like Jordan to make sure she was all right. He was the kind of man who took care of everyone and everything around him.

"If you're upset, I can't blame you," he said. "I dumped a heavy load on you out there today."

He was waiting. She took a deep breath. "I've been thinking, Jordan. Lucas loves it here and he's become attached to you. He'd be devastated if we had to leave."

"Are you reconsidering my proposal?" His attempt at lightness was betrayed by a catch in his voice.

"Not yet. But I'm curious about the kind of marriage you'd have in mind."

"Are you asking if I'd expect you to share my bed? Damned right I would. And no more sneaking off in the night. I'd want to see you there in the morning. Every morning."

"I see." Heat stirred, rising into in Angie's face.

"Another thing." He moved behind her, wrapping his arms around the blanket, drawing her close. "I take marriage vows seriously. You could count on me to be faithful. And to cherish and protect you and Lucas, for as long as I live."

His words made her melt a little, in spite of herself. When was the last time anyone had wanted to cherish and protect her? She forced herself to stay strong. "And if we couldn't make it work? What then?" All she wanted was to turn around and lose herself in his arms, but she had to keep her head.

"Then you'd be free to go. But I'd want to keep some connection with Lucas, maybe even partial custody."

"It all sounds so cold, so practical."

"We're practical people, Angie. And we both want the best for your boy. That's why I think we could make a good thing of this."

"What about your mother? If you married me, would she cut you out of the trust?"

He shook his head. "Right now I'm the only heir. And without my support, the ranch would have to be sold off. She'd never let that happen. As for her feelings about you, my mother's practical, too. She'd come around eventually, if only for her grandson's sake."

Angie closed her eyes, leaning back into his supporting warmth. *Practical—that's the word for it, Jordan,* she thought. *You've got this all figured out. But the bottom line is you don't love me. How am I supposed to live with that for the rest of my life?*

Jordan's arms tightened before he let her go. "There's time," he said. "Think about it. You've heard my conditions. I won't expect an answer till you're sure."

Would she ever be sure? Angie turned toward him, her eyes tracing the shadows that shaped his face. He was so like Justin, yet not like him at all.

And what about Justin's plane crash? Did Jordan ever plan to tell her how it had happened? Could she give him her answer without knowing?

She could sense the hunger in his gaze and feel the response stirring in her own body. She wanted him. But she couldn't go to him in turmoil. She needed time alone to clear her head and think things out. Hesitating, she took a step backward.

"I understand, Angie." He spoke as if he'd read her thoughts. "Tonight would just muddy the water. Let's give it a break for now. All right?"

She gazed up at him, aching to be held, kissed and reassured but knowing it would only make things harder. "Yes," she said. "That's a sensible idea. Good night, Jordan."

Thrusting the blanket at him, she turned away and hurried back inside. She had work to do, enough to occupy her mind until bedtime.

But even then, she'd be lucky to get much sleep.

Thirteen

Angie tossed and turned most of the night, replaying Jordan's proposal in her mind. *We're practical people.* That was how he'd described them both. But he was wrong. She wasn't practical at all. Jordan had offered her a life of privilege and material comforts. What he hadn't offered her were the things she truly wanted— honesty, openness and love.

Bless Uncle Jordan that he'll want to be my daddy. Bless us that we can live here forever.

Lucas's childish prayer had been so simple, so heartfelt. A word from her could give him what he wanted. He'd have two parents, a permanent home, everything Justin Cooper's son deserved. How could she deny him that for the sake of her own selfish needs? Wasn't this what Justin would want for Lucas?

The man was too drunk to walk a straight line, let alone fly a plane.

Victor's shattering news had tarnished her memory of Justin. But nothing could change the certainty that he'd loved her. She had no such certainty with Jordan. She didn't know how he felt about her, and she certainly didn't know why he'd kept the truth about Justin's death from her.

How could she trust a man who closed himself off and kept secrets from her? How could she spend her life with such a man?

She yearned for sleep. But when she closed her eyes it was Justin's face she saw, merging subtly into Jordan's, then back again. Gradually their features merged, becoming one and the same, blurring, fading into darkness until, at last, she slept.

When the dream came it was so vivid it could have been real. She was with Justin in his plane, her body strapped to the passenger seat. The moonlit night was calm and clear. But something wasn't right. The plane was rocking crazily, dipping and yawing as if battered by gale force winds. Rigid with fear, she gripped the armrests.

"Justin!" she shouted at the pilot. "What's wrong?"

He flashed her a devilish grin. "Just havin' a little fun, babe. You ain't seen nuthin' yet!"

Banking the plane sharply, he executed a heart-dropping barrel roll. Angie screamed as she found herself upside down. She'd never enjoyed wild carnival rides, and this was ten times worse because it was so dangerous. Her stomach lurched as they came upright again. The air in the cockpit smelled of whiskey. "Please, Justin," she begged. "I'm getting sick. Let's just land and go home."

His laugh had a manic quality. "So, are you going to tell me what you did with my brother? Was it as good as with me? Maybe better?"

"You don't know what you're..." Her words ended in

a cry as Justin pulled back hard on the stick, sending the plane into a dizzying climb.

She knew what was going to happen next. She'd watched from the ground, heart in her throat, as Justin did loops in his plane, climbing almost out of sight, then somersaulting backward into a long, flashing dive. Just when she feared he was about to crash into the ground he'd pull out and shoot upward again. It was terrifying enough to watch, and now she was in the plane.

"Don't do this, Justin," she pleaded as the plane roared skyward. "I'm going to have a baby! *Our* baby!"

He shot her a glance of sudden clarity, but it was too late to pull out of the loop. Angie screamed as the plane arced backward and streaked into its dive. She could see the ground rushing up at them. "Pull out, Justin!" she shouted. "Pull out now!"

At the last second he pulled back on the stick. Miraculously, the plane leveled off and began to climb again. Angie breathed a silent prayer. Justin knew about the baby. He'd be careful now. They were going to be all right.

Suddenly the mountain loomed ahead of them, huge and black, blocking out the stars. She had no time to cry out before the world exploded, ending everything.

Angie woke drenched in sweat. For a few moments she lay still, her heart hammering. She'd had a nightmare; that was all. She was alive, her son safe in the next room. Justin had died alone, nearly four years ago.

But the dream had changed something. As Angie stared up into the darkness she realized she'd waited long enough. She needed to know the truth behind Justin's accident—now. And the only person who could tell her was asleep downstairs.

Swinging her feet to the floor she reached for her robe.

Jordan might refuse to answer her questions. But Angie had made up her mind. She'd give him no rest until she'd heard the entire story—all of it.

Stepping into Lucas's room, she gazed down at her sleeping son. Someday he'd want to know how his father had died. What she was about to do was for him and for herself.

Jordan groaned and opened his eyes. Angie's pale face, framed by tousled waves of black hair, swam into focus above him. "What is it?" he muttered. "Is Lucas all right?"

"Lucas is fine. But we need to talk."

"Lord, it's—" He switched on the bedside lamp and glanced at the clock. "It's almost 3:30 in the morning, woman. Can't we wait for a more civilized hour?"

She shook her head. "I've already waited too long. This conversation needs to happen now."

Sobered by her tone, Jordan sat up and raked a hand through his hair. "I can make coffee."

"Don't bother." She sat on the foot of the bed, tucking her bare feet beneath her robe. The faint light cast her dark eyes into pools of shadow. "I just had a dream—an awful dream about Justin's plane crash. You were in Park City when he died. I want to know what happened. Everything. Now."

A knot had formed in the pit of Jordan's stomach. "It's been almost four years. Why bring it up now? What's this about, Angie?"

"It's about us. About trust." She fingered a fold in the quilt. "My cousin checked the accident report for me. I know Justin was drunk when he crashed. What else did you hide from me, Jordan?"

The knot twisted and tightened. "Does it matter? You

and my parents were in enough pain. I wanted to spare you more."

"Did you ever plan to tell me?"

"No."

"It's that bad?"

"It's past history. None of us can change it. Forget it and go back to bed."

"It's too late for that," she said. "I'm not leaving this room until you tell me everything."

So it had come to this—the moment he'd hoped would never happen. Jordan began the story, knowing Angie deserved the truth—and knowing that once she'd heard it she would walk away from him and never look back.

"The ski trip was a bad idea from the beginning," he said. "When we weren't on the slopes all we did was argue."

"About me."

He exhaled wearily. "Justin was reckless and impulsive. I honestly felt it was my duty to protect him from making a bad decision."

"Of course." Angie glanced down at her clasped hands. Jordan had never made a secret of his disapproval. She'd have expected nothing less of him.

"We'd planned to fly back the morning of your birthday. The night before, in the room, I pushed him too far and we got into the nastiest fight of our lives. He swore at me, called me a meddling bastard. He shouted that you were the only one who really loved him, and the rest of the family could rot in hell for all he cared."

Jordan paused to clear his throat. "It was too much. I lost control. And I did something I'll regret to the end of my days."

Jordan's anguish hung like a black curtain between

them. Angie could feel it in the ragged breath he drew before he continued.

"That New Year's Eve when I drove you home in my car— I told him about it, Angie. I told him…everything."

Angie stared at him in horror. The words spilled from her lips. "How…could…you?"

"How many times do you think I've asked myself that question?" His voice was a growl. "At the time I rationalized that it was for his own good, that I was helping him by trying to split the two of you up. But looking back, I can't help wondering if—" He bit back the rest of the words, shaking his head.

"If what? Tell me."

"I can't help wondering if I did it because I wanted you for myself."

"Jordan—"

"Don't say a word. I'm the king of hypocrites, and I know it. Now, do you want to hear the rest of the story, or don't you?"

"I don't want to," Angie whispered. "But I need to. Go on."

Again, he cleared his throat. When he spoke, the words sounded flat, like a confession extracted by torture. "Justin reacted by slugging me so hard it knocked me down. By the time I got to my feet he was out the door. I figured he'd gone to blow off some steam, so I didn't go after him. If I had, I wouldn't be telling this story." Jordan raked his hair with agitated fingers. "The hotel bartender said he'd called Justin a cab, and that he'd left drunk, saying he was going to have it out with some woman. Nobody saw him take off from the airport in Heber, but someone reported the flash when the plane hit the mountain. That's all I know."

He fell silent, looking utterly drained. Reliving the

story of Justin's death had to be one of the most painful things he'd ever done, and it showed. His face was drawn, his hands clenched on his knees.

Angie sat frozen. Part of her yearned to take Jordan in her arms and hold him, comforting them both. But another, stronger part had no desire to touch or be touched. She was too stunned to feel.

"It was never your fault, Angie," Jordan said. "Of all my sins, one of the worst was letting you blame yourself."

Angie found her voice. "But it *was* my fault. And it was your fault, too. That night in your car, when we couldn't keep our hands off each other, we set this whole tragedy in motion."

"You can't think like that. Was it my parents' fault for giving us that ski trip? Was it the cab driver's fault for leaving Justin at the airport?"

"That's enough." Angie felt as if the life had been sucked from her limbs. "I can't do this anymore, Jordan. I can't be with you."

He made no move to stop her as she rose and walked out of the room. Raquel had been right. Everything Jordan had done for her and her son—bringing them here, giving them a home, trying to make Lucas his brother's heir, even asking her to marry him—had been driven by guilt.

More guilt than she could live with.

And not just his guilt. She meant what she'd said—it had been her fault, too. She was the one who had given in to Jordan's kiss in the car all those years ago. And she was the one who had fallen for him now. Everything that they'd shared since she'd moved into the ranch...none of it would have been possible if it hadn't been for that single betrayal that triggered it all.

Shivering through her robe, she crossed the parlor and dragged herself up the stairs. There was no way she could stay here. Looking at Jordan every day and remembering what he'd done—not just in the way he'd pushed Justin over the edge, but also how he'd kept it from her—would tear her apart.

Lucas would be distraught, but letting him take Rudy would ease things. And Raquel had a guest room where they could stay while she looked for a new place. It wouldn't be easy, but somehow she would make a good life for herself and her son.

Jordan would want to keep seeing Lucas, of course, and Lucas would want it, too. She would have to live with that. But every time she saw him, she would remind herself of the reasons she'd left. And she would bury the memory of being in Jordan's arms, holding him close as he shattered inside her.

Moonlight shone through her bedroom window. It was still night outside, but she was too rattled to sleep. Pulling on her jeans and sweatshirt, she flung open the closet and started packing.

Jordan was up at first light, filling a cup with hot coffee to sip as he walked out to the barn. There was no sign of Angie. But that was for the best. After last night a face-to-face encounter would be painful for them both.

She was leaving. He knew it in his bones, and he didn't want to be around when it happened.

After finishing his coffee, he saddled the palomino, mounted and headed for the foothills behind the ranch. His breath frosted the air but he was dressed for the weather in his sheepskin coat. Before long the sun would be up to warm the land and brighten the day.

Jordan felt no brightness as he nudged the horse to a canter. Only now did he realize how much hope he'd staked on marrying Angie and raising her son. In the past weeks, they'd added an element of family to his life. He'd looked forward to coming home, hearing Lucas's happy shout as the little boy raced to meet him. He'd warmed with anticipation at the thought of Angie in his bed, her loving body in his arms, her silky black hair spilling over his pillow.

Now it was over. The scandal was out, and Angie had responded exactly the way he'd expected. He'd done the unforgiveable by telling Justin about that stolen moment in his car. Angie would probably hate him forever. But at least he had nothing else to hide. The secret that had kept him prisoner was a secret no more.

In an ironic sort of way, he was free.

Pausing on a ridge, he looked back toward the ranch. Marta's brown Honda was pulling into its place behind the kitchen. Except for the horses in the corral and a curl of smoke from the bunkhouse, there was no other sign of activity.

He would give Angie plenty of time—to leave, to think things over, or whatever the hell she was going to do. Being there might tempt him to say too much.

And what would he say?

That he loved her?

That he'd be miserable without her?

Would it do any good?

He crested the hill and rode up toward the line where piñon and juniper met forests of white-trunked aspen. The sunlit trees glistened with frost. A startled red-tailed hawk flapped off its kill. He thought of Angie and how he'd wanted to share mornings like this with her. Now he never would.

For another hour he rode along the base of the mountains. Then, finding no peace, he turned for home.

Marta was waiting for him when he walked in. If her

dark eyes had been bullets, Jordan would have needed a medic. "They're gone," she said. "They packed up the car and drove away after breakfast. They even took the dog. What did you do to her?"

"She didn't tell you?"

"She wasn't talking. But the boy was in tears. How could you let that woman get away?"

Jordan stared at his housekeeper in surprise. "I thought you didn't like her."

"Not at first. But then I saw what a good mother she was and how she made you happy. I know you're my boss, but I have to say it. You're a fool to let her go!"

The words struck Jordan like a slap. "Believe me, it wasn't my idea. Did she say anything at all?"

"Not about you. Just that she left a letter. In there." She pointed in the direction of Jordan's office.

Jordan walked down the hall on leaden feet. Whatever Angie had written, reading it wouldn't be pleasant.

The letter was on his desk in a sealed envelope. Tearing it open he unfolded the single, typewritten sheet and began to read.

> Dear Jordan,
> By the time you read this, Lucas and I will be gone. I apologize for taking the car. As soon as I can get it refinanced, I plan to send you the money.

As if he cared about the fool car! Fighting the temptation to crush the letter in his fist, Jordan read on.

> I appreciate all you've done for us. And thank you for telling me how the crash came about. Taking Lucas away from the ranch was one of the hardest decisions I've

ever made. But you and I could never be
happy together. Remembering how our actions led to Justin's death would wear us
both down, leaving nothing but bitterness.

  I know better than to try and hide from
you. You have the means to find us anywhere. And I haven't the heart to deny you
the right to see Lucas. Once we're settled,
you're welcome to arrange some time with
him. He would like that. But please don't
expect anything more from me. I'll be doing
my best to build a new life—without you.
Sincerely,
Angie

Sincerely! Jordan swore out loud. Not a word of affection from the woman. Nothing about what they'd been to
each other. Jordan crumpled Angie's letter and spiked it
into the wastebasket. A moment later, still scowling, he
fished it out, smoothed it flat and slid it under the blotter
on his desk. Marta had been right. He should never have
let her go. He should have fallen on his knees, begged,
bribed, threatened, done whatever it took to keep her here.

  He needed her. He loved her.

  But he'd learned that too late.

Fourteen

Angie hadn't planned to tell her cousin the story behind Justin's crash. But Raquel's gentle persistence could pry secrets out of a stone. The two of them sat at the kitchen table, sipping spiced *chocolate* as their sons romped with the dog on the patio.

"But how can you blame yourself, *querida?*" Raquel asked. "And how can you blame Jordan? Did either of you force Justin to get drunk? Did you drive him to the airport and shove him into that plane?"

Angie shook her head. "But what if I could have kept it from happening? Maybe if I hadn't waited so long to tell him I was pregnant—"

Raquel put her cup down with a thud. "Listen to your cousin, even though you might not want to hear this. I always thought Justin was a sweet but spoiled little boy. He did what he wanted, and you were always making excuses for him. You're still making excuses."

"But he was so upset when Jordan told him what we'd done—"

"See what I mean? Yes, Jordan should have kept that story to himself. He made a mistake. But he didn't know what kind of crazy thing Justin would do. Nobody could have known."

Angie gulped back the ache in her throat. "You're saying I should forgive Jordan?"

"Forgive him?" Raquel pulled a tissue from a box on the table. "Well, that depends. Do you think he kept the secret for selfish reasons because he didn't want to take responsibility for what he had done?"

"No," Angie answered without hesitation. Jordan was the last man on Earth to shirk his responsibilities. "I think he wanted to spare his parents and keep Justin's memory from getting tarnished."

"If he'd told his parents the truth, do you think they would have blamed him?"

Angie snorted. "Of course not. They'd have blamed me."

Raquel nodded. "Right. So, in conclusion, to protect his parents and you, Jordan carried that awful burden alone for years, not telling a soul because he didn't want anyone else to feel the pain he was feeling. Then he told you, and instead of giving him comfort, you ran away. Don't you think he's been punished enough?"

Angie felt the tears break loose inside her. This time she couldn't hold them back. Her words were broken by sobs. She'd felt so hurt, so wronged by Jordan's actions. How could she have presumed to judge him? How could she expect him to ever forgive her? "It's too late. Jordan's such a proud man. After the things I said to him…"

"Here, *chica.*" Raquel pressed a fresh tissue into her hand. "Go ahead and cry. Get it out."

Angie dabbed at her streaming eyes. "The worst part is, I love him, Raquel. I love him so much, and now he'll never take me back."

"Mama?"

Angie glanced up. A forlorn little figure stood in the kitchen doorway. "Are you all right, Mama?" Lucas asked.

Angie blinked away furious tears. "I'll be fine, sweetheart. Run and play."

Casting a worried look at his mother, Lucas turned and trotted back to the patio.

Jordan pulled into the ranch driveway, head aching after an emotional hour with his mother. The decision to tell her about Justin's drunken flight had been painful, but now that the story was known, and might spread, he'd wanted her to hear it from him.

He'd spared her the part about kissing Angie in his car. That was private and personal. It was enough to say that he and Justin had had a roaring fight in Park City, and Justin had gone off angry enough to get drunk.

Meredith had taken the news with her usual icy calm. But Jordan had known she was hurting. Justin had been her favorite. She'd never made a secret of that.

"How could he do such a thing when we loved him so much?" Jordan had detected a slight break in her voice.

"He didn't mean to, Mother. He was out of control."

"And you've known all this time."

"I thought it would be a kindness to keep it to myself. Was I wrong?"

"Does it matter now? Your brother's gone, and nothing's going to bring him back."

In a rare move, Jordan had risen, walked to his mother's chair and laid a hand on her shoulder. Meredith had never been physically affectionate with her sons, but she'd surprised him by tilting her head to press her cheek to his fingers.

"Justin was like your father," she'd said. "Maybe that's why I loved him so much. You're more like me, keeping everything under control. I've counted on you for that."

For the first time, Jordan had realized it was true.

"I suppose you've told Angelina," she'd said as he moved away.

"Yes. She took it hard. But at least she knows the crash wasn't her fault. It's time you knew it, too. She's taken far too much of the blame."

"I know. After seeing her with that man in La Fonda, I asked my lawyer to check her background. He found nothing to suggest that she's anything but honest, hardworking and a good mother. I still had my doubts, but the last time you were here, after you walked out on me, I did some soul-searching. How could you defend her so passionately if she wasn't worthy of it? I don't often admit to being wrong, but I fear I've misjudged her. I'd very much like to make amends in person."

"I'm afraid that won't be easy. She's gone. Packed up Lucas and the dog and left the ranch yesterday morning."

"And you didn't stop her? What were you thinking?"

"Angie wasn't a prisoner. She had every right to leave—and to take her son with her."

Meredith had given him a look he hadn't seen since his boyhood. "Well, for heaven's sake, go after them! Do you want some love in your life, or would you rather end up a cranky, controlling old pain-in-the-derriere like me?"

Now, as Jordan gulped down two aspirins, he recalled his mother's startling advice. Meredith Cooper was not a stupid woman. What she'd told him was right on the mark. But what he'd done—not just to Justin but also to

Angie, in keeping the truth from her for all this time—was unforgiveable. Now that she knew, how could he have any hope of getting her back?

At least Angie was willing to let him see Lucas. Push her too far and even that could be snatched away. Better to leave well enough alone.

He still planned to make the boy Justin's heir. Now that his mother was reconciled, that should be easy enough. And he would set up a fund to pay for Lucas's education and anything else he needed. But Angie was no longer part of the package. She'd declared that she couldn't be with him. End of story.

Wandering into his office, he surveyed the empty stillness.

The books and everything else had been left in immaculate order. But, damn it, he missed the cheerful chaos of Angie, Lucas and that fool dog. He missed the laughter. He missed the warmth. What was he going to do without them?

His thoughts were interrupted by the jangling of the landline phone on the desk. Strange, most people would've called on his cell. He picked up the receiver.

"Hello?"

"Uncle Jordan?" His heart lurched at the sound of the childish voice.

"Lucas! How did you get this number?"

"It's on Rudy's collar. I tried to call you before but you weren't there."

"Where are you? Are you all right?"

"We're at Raquel's. Mama was crying. She told Raquel she loves you. I think she wants to come back. I do, too."

Jordan forced himself to breathe. "Did your mother tell you to call me?"

"No."

"Where is she?"

"In the kitchen. She can't hear me."

"So she doesn't know you called." Lord, what now?

"Can you come and get us?"

"I don't know yet. Listen, Lucas, hang up the phone and don't say anything. I'll see what I can do."

"Promise?"

"I said I'd see." By the time he hung up, Jordan was already having doubts. He knew where Angie's cousin lived. But he couldn't just go charging over there and make a fool of himself, could he?

What if Lucas's story was a little boy's fantasy?

What if Angie didn't really want him?

But even as he weighed his excuses, Jordan was reaching for his keys and striding out the door and down to driveway to his car.

Angie was at the kitchen table, scanning the rental section of the *Santa Fe Sentinel* when the doorbell rang.

"I'll get it!" Raquel bustled through the kitchen and vanished into the parlor. Angie heard muted voices. Probably a salesman. She went back to circling ads for the few places that allowed pets.

Moments later Raquel appeared in the kitchen doorway, a mysterious glint in her eyes. An unaccustomed prickle stole up the back of Angie's neck.

"Who was at the door?" she asked.

"No one of importance, *querida*. Why? Did you think it might be Jordan?"

The name tightened a knot around her heart. "Stop teasing me, Raquel. He doesn't even know we're here."

"What if it *had* been Jordan? What would you have done?"

Angie shrugged, feigning indifference. "Does it matter?"

"It does if you love him. And you said you did."

Angie looked up from the newspaper. "Will you stop this? I *do* love him. And I know I've made a mistake. But Jordan's a proud man. He wouldn't take me back if I begged him on my knees."

"Would you forgive him?"

Tears welled in Angie's eyes. "What are you trying to do? Look, you're making me cry again. Of course, I'd forgive him. I already have. But it's too late. So leave me alone."

What was wrong with Raquel? She was actually grinning.

The creak of the opening patio door broke into Angie's thoughts. Lucas and Rudy had come into the kitchen. Suddenly the dog's head shot up. Yipping with joy, he bolted through the kitchen and into the parlor with Lucas right behind him.

"Uncle Jordan!" Lucas flung himself at the tall figure who'd stepped into sight, fending off Rudy's wild greeting. "You came!"

Overwhelmed, Angie pressed her hands to her burning face. She was dimly aware of Raquel ushering Lucas and his pet out of the room and closing the door.

"Angie." He stood behind her, his hands resting on her shoulders. His touch sent a quiver through her body. "Say the word and I'll go."

She shook her head, forcing the words past the tightness in her throat. "Don't go," she whispered.

"I won't. Not unless you and Lucas go with me." Easing her to her feet, he pulled her against him. His arms cradled her close.

"I'm sorry," she murmured against his chest. "I had no right to judge what you did in the past."

"And I had no right to keep secrets from the woman I love. There'll be no more, I promise."

Angie pulled away a little. Her pulse thundered as she gazed up at him. "Did I just hear what I think I heard?"

His chuckle was tinged with raw emotion. "I love you, Angelina Montoya," he said. "I love every stubborn, feisty, beautiful inch of you. And I'm not leaving this house until you promise to come back—for good."

Angie's throat welled. "You're sure that's what you want? A lifetime of chaos? Because that's what you'll be getting."

He laughed again, a glorious sound to her ears. "I want the whole package—you, Lucas, that fool mutt and all the babies I can give you." His arms tightened. "I should probably propose, but as I recall, I've already done that. How about an answer, lady?"

"You need to ask?"

"I'm asking."

"Then it's yes. A hundred times yes." She pulled him down to her in a long, deep kiss as the kitchen door opened and the two eavesdroppers burst in.

"We couldn't wait any longer," Raquel said, hugging them both.

Lucas tugged at Jordan's pant leg. "Uncle Jordan, can I call you Daddy now?"

A family had begun.

Epilogue

One year later...

"Here's your little girl, Mrs. Cooper." The nurse handed Angie a sleepy, pink-wrapped bundle. Overcome with love, Angie snuggled her newborn close, filling her senses with her warmth and sweet baby scent. Her hand folded back the blanket to show the puckered rosebud face and silky black curls.

"She looks just like you," Jordan said.

"Not quite. Look at that dimple in her cheek and the way her hair sticks up in back. She's a Cooper all right. She'll probably be as strong-willed as her father."

"My two beautiful girls. I'll be busting my buttons with pride." Jordan brushed a fingertip over the baby's hair, then bent over the bed and kissed his wife tenderly on the lips. He'd proved himself a firm but loving father to Lucas and she had no doubt he would be the same to his daughter.

"Do you want to hold her?" Angie asked. "She won't break, you know."

"Hey, I held her in the delivery room and did fine. Give me my girl." He slipped his hands under the baby and eased her to his shoulder. She settled against him with a little cooing sound. The man was a natural.

Their first year of marriage had been a time of adjustment, but their deep love had eased the way. Angie had insisted on continuing her web design business and had added some on-line university courses to her schedule. One day she hoped to become a teacher. But these precious years while her children were young would be spent at home with them.

Lucas had been added to the family trust as Justin's heir. He'd also been adopted as Jordan's son. Someday he stood to be the head of the growing Cooper family and a very rich man, but for now nothing was more important than having a mother and father who loved him—and who loved each other.

"Where is she? I want to see my granddaughter!" The door of the hospital room swung open and Meredith strode in with Lucas bounding ahead of her. Being a grandma had transformed Jordan's mother. She doted on Lucas and had been over the moon about the baby.

"Big brother first," Jordan said, sitting so Lucas could see and touch the baby. "Here she is, son, your little sister."

Lucas touched the baby's cheek with a tentative finger. His eyes lit as his mouth spread in a grin. "She's soft," he said. "What's her name?"

"Her name is Selena," Angie said. "Selena Meredith Cooper for her two grandmothers."

"Oh! Oh, my goodness!" Tears had sprung to Meredith's eyes and were rolling down her cheeks. It was like watching a marble statue break into weeping. "Let me have her." She all but snatched the baby up, cradling her in eager arms. "My little angel," she crooned. "I can hardly wait to take you shopping!"

Angie felt Jordan's hand close around hers. The Coopers were a clan of powerful personalities. Life in this family would never be dull.

A light touch, barely perceptible, brushed her cheek. Angie turned her head. No one was there but she sensed a warm presence in the room. She couldn't be sure, of course, but something told her that, if Justin was really there, he was smiling.

* * * * *

COMING NEXT MONTH from Harlequin Desire®
AVAILABLE FEBRUARY 5, 2013

#2209 THE KING NEXT DOOR
Kings of California
Maureen Child
Griffin King has strict rules about getting involved with a single mother, but temptation is right next door.

#2210 BEDROOM DIPLOMACY
Daughters of Power: The Capital
Michelle Celmer
A senator's daughter ends up as a bargaining chip that could divert a besotted diplomat's attention to marriage negotiations instead!

#2211 A REAL COWBOY
Rich, Rugged Ranchers
Sarah M. Anderson
He's given up Hollywood for his ranch and doesn't want to go back. How far will she go to sign him to the role of a lifetime?

#2212 MARRIAGE WITH BENEFITS
Winner of Harlequin's 2011 SYTYCW contest
Kat Cantrell
Cia Allende needs a husband—so she can divorce him and gain her trust fund. She doesn't expect that the man she's handpicked will become someone she can't live without.

#2213 ALL HE REALLY NEEDS
At Cain's Command
Emily McKay
When lovers must suddenly work together to unravel a mystery from his family's past, their private affair threatens to become very public.

#2214 A TRICKY PROPOSITION
Cat Schield
When Ming asks her best friend to help her become a mother, he persuades her to conceive the old-fashioned way. But will his brother—Ming's ex-fiancé—stand in the way?

REQUEST YOUR FREE BOOKS!
2 FREE NOVELS PLUS 2 FREE GIFTS!

(H) HARLEQUIN® *Desire*

ALWAYS POWERFUL, PASSIONATE AND PROVOCATIVE

YES! Please send me 2 FREE Harlequin Desire® novels and my 2 FREE gifts (gifts are worth about $10). After receiving them, if I don't wish to receive any more books, I can return the shipping statement marked "cancel." If I don't cancel, I will receive 6 brand-new novels every month and be billed just $4.30 per book in the U.S. or $4.99 per book in Canada. That's a savings of at least 14% off the cover price! It's quite a bargain! Shipping and handling is just 50¢ per book in the U.S. and 75¢ per book in Canada.* I understand that accepting the 2 free books and gifts places me under no obligation to buy anything. I can always return a shipment and cancel at any time. Even if I never buy another book, the two free books and gifts are mine to keep forever.

225/326 HDN FVP7

Name	(PLEASE PRINT)

Address		Apt. #

City	State/Prov.	Zip/Postal Code

Signature (if under 18, a parent or guardian must sign)

Mail to the **Harlequin® Reader Service:**
IN U.S.A.: P.O. Box 1867, Buffalo, NY 14240-1867
IN CANADA: P.O. Box 609, Fort Erie, Ontario L2A 5X3

Want to try two free books from another line?
Call 1-800-873-8635 or visit www.ReaderService.com.

* Terms and prices subject to change without notice. Prices do not include applicable taxes. Sales tax applicable in N.Y. Canadian residents will be charged applicable taxes. Offer not valid in Quebec. This offer is limited to one order per household. Not valid for current subscribers to Harlequin Desire books. All orders subject to credit approval. Credit or debit balances in a customer's account(s) may be offset by any other outstanding balance owed by or to the customer. Please allow 4 to 6 weeks for delivery. Offer available while quantities last.

Your Privacy—The Harlequin® Reader Service is committed to protecting your privacy. Our Privacy Policy is available online at www.ReaderService.com or upon request from the Harlequin Reader Service.

We make a portion of our mailing list available to reputable third parties that offer products we believe may interest you. If you prefer that we not exchange your name with third parties, or if you wish to clarify or modify your communication preferences, please visit us at www.ReaderService.com/consumerschoice or write to us at Harlequin Reader Service Preference Service, P.O. Box 9062, Buffalo, NY 14269. Include your complete name and address.

HD13

Dial up the passion to Red-Hot with the Harlequin Blaze series!

NEW LOOK COMING DEC 18!

Harlequin Blaze stories sizzle with strong heroines and irresistible heroes playing the game of modern love and lust. They're fun, sexy and always steamy.

HARLEQUIN®

Blaze

Red-Hot Reads

www.Harlequin.com

HBPOST

Navy SEAL Blake Landon joins this year's
parade of *Uniformly Hot!* military heroes in
Tawny Weber's

A SEAL's Seduction

Blake's lips brushed over Alexia's and she forgot that they were
on a public beach. His breath was warm, his lips soft.

The fingertips he traced over her shoulder were like a gentle
whisper. It was sweetness personified. She felt like a fairy-tale
princess being kissed for the first time by her prince.

And he was delicious.

Mouthwatering, heart-stopping delicious. And clearly he
had no problem going after what he wanted, she realized as he
slid the tips of his fingers over the bare skin of her shoulder.
Alexia shivered at the contrast of his hard fingertips against
her skin. Her breath caught as his hand shifted, sliding lower,
hinting at but not actually caressing the upper swell of her
breast.

Her heart pounded so hard against her throat, she was surprised it didn't jump right out into his hand.

She wanted him. As she'd never wanted another man in
her life. For years, she'd behaved. She'd carefully considered
her actions, making sure she didn't hurt others. She'd poured
herself into her career, into making sure her life was one she
was proud of.

And she already had a man who wanted her in his life. A nice, sweet man she could talk through the night with and never run out of things to say.

But she wanted more.

She wanted a man who'd keep her up all night. Who'd drive her wild, sending her body to places she'd never even dreamed of.

Even if it was only for one night.

And that, she realized, was the key. One night of crazy. One night of delicious, empowered, indulge-her-every-desire sex, with a man who made her melt.

One night would be incredible.

One night would *have* to be enough.

Pick up *A SEAL's Seduction* by Tawny Weber, on sale January 22.

Rediscover the Harlequin series section starting December 18!

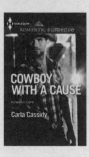